I0639492

David Garrick

The Life of Mr. James Quin

comedian, with the History of the Stage From His Commencing Actor to

His Retreat to Bath

David Garrick

The Life of Mr. James Quin
comedian, with the History of the Stage From His Commencing Actor to His Retreat to Bath

ISBN/EAN: 9783744769204

Printed in Europe, USA, Canada, Australia, Japan

Cover: Foto ©Raphael Reischuk / pixelio.de

More available books at **www.hansebooks.com**

PREFATORY NOTE.

The first portion of the following work is a reprint of the exceedingly scarce life of James Quin, published in 1766.

This actor was a man who reached such a high standard of excellence in his profession, and who consequently acquired such an enviable celebrity, being surpassed, or at any rate equalled, by one other comedian only of his time, his fellow-performer at the same theatre, David Garrick, that it is confidently believed the reproduction of a work now rarely to be met with will be welcome in dramatic and other circles.

Facilities for printing not being as great a century ago as they are now, there is frequently a great paucity of material for the compilation of a biographical sketch. Efforts, however, have now been made to collect, in the form of an appendix, fragmentary notices scattered in various directions, in order to add them to the work in question, and, as far as possible, render it complete.

From the author's words in his opening chapter, there appears to have been special difficulty in the accomplishment of this particular task, "the Histories of the Stage," he remarks, "scarcely mentioning Quin, either as an actor or as a man," so that what he had to offer to the reader was "principally gathered from conversation and acquaintance." He hopes, however, he says, "that from these materials and such other as he can obtain, some future biographer may transmit to posterity this actor's memory."

The publisher of this book submits it to the collector as an attempt to fulfil the above.

THE LIFE OF

MR. JAMES QUIN

COMEDIAN,

WITH THE

HISTORY OF THE STAGE

FROM

HIS COMMENCING ACTOR TO HIS RETREAT TO BATH.

ILLUSTRATED WITH MANY

Curious and Interesting Anecdotes

OF SEVERAL

PERSONS OF DISTINCTION, LITERATURE, AND GALLANTRY.

TO WHICH IS ADDED A

SUPPLEMENT

OF

ORIGINAL FACTS AND ANECDOTES,

ARRANGED FROM AUTHENTIC SOURCES.

TOGETHER WITH HIS

TRIAL FOR THE MURDER OF MR. BOWEN.

———

LONDON.

1887.

THE LIFE OF

MR. JAMES QUIN

COMEDIAN,

WITH THE

HISTORY OF THE STAGE

FROM

HIS COMMENCING ACTOR TO HIS RETREAT TO BATH.

ILLUSTRATED WITH MANY

CURIOUS AND INTERESTING ANECDOTES

OF SEVERAL

PERSONS OF DISTINCTION, LITERATURE, AND GALLANTRY.

TO WHICH IS ADDED A

Genuine and Authentic Copy of his Last Will and Testament.

———

DEDICATED TO DAVID GARRICK, ESQ.

———

London:

PRINTED FOR S. BLADON, IN PATERNOSTER ROW

1766.

TO

DAVID GARRICK, ESQ.

WHOSE patronage, sir, can these sheets more properly claim than yours? The Life of Mr. Quin is so immediately connected with your own, and his pursuits for a long time were so very similar, that no one can form so just an estimate of the man, or judge so well of the merits of the actor, as he who is at once the real representative and the only just commentator of Shakespeare. Permit me therefore, sir, to lay this little work at your feet, which I flatter myself, if not from its intrinsic worth, at least from the subject, you will deign to accept of, and place among those volumes which illustrate dramatic history. I am, sir,

Amongst many thousands,

Your constant admirer,

And most obedient humble servant,

THE EDITOR.

The Life of
Mr. James Quin, Comedian.

CHAPTER I.

His birth, family, expectancies, studies, early pursuits. The reason of changing them. His future plan of life interrupted by a very uncommon and almost fatal adventure—with its sequel.

THE public will, it is imagined, not be displeased to have some account of a person of whom so much has been said, and of whom so little has been hitherto known. His jokes may be called the standing jests of the town; but those who have hackneyed some of them, and murdered others, have scarce ever entered into the most cursory part of his life and character; and yet, according to Mr. Addison, the best story in the world loses its greatest poignancy when we are unacquainted with its hero. This, amongst other considerations, induced the editor of this performance to attempt an essay towards the Life of Mr. James Quin, in hopes that some future biographer may from these materials, and such others as he can obtain, transmit to posterity the memory of a man who has diverted the present age in public and in private—upon the dramatic stage as well as that of life; who was one of the best actors and most facetious men of his time;—who was at once the gentleman and the scholar—the philosopher and the critic—the humourist and the moral man, the scourge of knaves and fools, and the admiration of the sensible and good. Such are the outlines of the picture before us; in every respect an original, and indeed inimitable, yet not without defects and blemishes in some of the features and in various parts of the drapery. Perfection is not the lot of humanity, and an honest historian scorns to flatter.

In the pursuit of this task the editor has encountered many difficulties, as there are scarce any lights to be met with in such books as might be supposed to give some anecdotes of so extraordinary a character. The Histories of the Stage, the Annals of the Theatre, scarce mention him either as an actor or a man, so that what is here offered to the reader is principally gathered from conversation and acquaintance.

It might look somewhat too pompous to say that, like Homer, more than one city claimed his birth, yet this is really true; for though it has been generally believed that he drew his first breath in Dublin, other parts of Ireland have been mentioned as the place of his nativity. He was, however, born in the parish of St. Paul, Covent Garden, London, in the year 1693. Various also are the reports of his family. Some have averred that his father was an American, and that James was the illegitimate issue of a criminal correspondence, which his father kept up in Ireland upon his return from the western hemisphere, and that on this account he was deprived of his patrimonial expectations. This imaginary lineage was never allowed by Quin himself; on the contrary, he always asserted that his father was an English gentleman, who, some years after his son's birth, settled in Ireland, and was possessed of a small fortune, which his natural generosity and beneficence greatly incumbered. James's education was such as suited the station which seemed to be allotted for him, that of a gentleman. After having gone through the necessary prelude of grammar-school learning he was sent to the university of Dublin, where he remained till he was over twenty years of age.

His father destined him for the bar, and at this period he came over to England to pursue his studies in jurisprudence. To this end he took chambers in the Temple, and for some time studied Coke upon Littleton with the usual success of young Templars, who consider their situation, so particularly adapted for pleasure, as no way compatible with so dry and tedious an application. A life of gaiety and dissipation took place, and he found a much stronger disposition to read Shakespeare than the statutes at large.

About this time his father died, when he found his patrimony so very small that there was no possibility of his supporting himself upon it; and this naturally induced him to begin seriously to think of availing himself of those talents which nature had bestowed upon him, and repairing by his own merit the effects of his father's generosity and too liberal hospitality. His good sense soon pointed out to him that as he had made but a very small progress in the study of the law, so he could not expect to reap the fruits of his present pursuit but at a very distant period; a young counsellor of the greatest merit has many obstacles to surmount before he obtains any considerable practice; chance and interest are great auxiliaries to his success, as many a veteran barrister has much reason to complain. Besides, his finances were so circumscribed that there was scarce a practicability of his accomplishing himself in this profession without some temporary support.

These reasons soon induced him to quit his present pursuit, and there appeared to him nowhere so fair a prospect as the stage. He had many requisites to form a good actor: an expressive countenance; a marking eye; a clear voice, full and melodious; an extensive memory, founded upon a long application to our best classic authors; an enthusiastic admiration of Shakespeare; a happy and articulate pronunciation; and a majestic figure. He had for some time associated with most of the capital actors of this period; he was frequently in company with Booth and Wilks, and formed a very strict intimacy with Ryan. It was to the last of these that he opened his mind with respect to coming upon the stage. Ryan was charmed to find his friend so sincerely approve of his plan of life as to be desirous of adopting it, and he introduced him to the managers of the Theatre Royal in Drury Lane, who engaged him in August 1717, to appear the succeeding winter.

How uncertain are the events of this transitory world! Quin, who was now assiduously employed in studying several parts, in which he imagined he might appear in the ensuing season, was, by a most unexpected incident obliged to leave this metropolis and take refuge in Ireland. Whoever was acquainted with our hero in his younger days must be sensible that he was of a very amorous disposition, and that James laid claim to no extravagant share of chastity. James carried on what he thought a very snug intrigue with Mrs. L———, a woollen draper's lady in the Strand. We shall pass over the various scenes of this growing correspondence, as they were usually represented at his own chambers; but the blind goddess was at length resolved to make him severely pay for all his good fortune. He had lent the key of his chambers to a friend of his. Quin accidentally met with Mrs. L———, who had been to the playhouse and could not get in. The opportunity was so favourable it was not to be slighted; he had already insisted upon her company, when it was too late to tell her he had just recollected he was not possessed of the key of his chambers; such an excuse would now have looked like coolness on his part. In a word, he prevailed on her, with much intreaty, to go to a bagnio, which was, perhaps, the first time in her life she had been in such a place. Her terrors were extravagantly great, till she thought there was no further danger to be apprehended, and gave a full loose to the indulgence of her passion. The hour of retreat now approached, when suddenly an ignorant waiter opened the door to introduce another company, not knowing the room was already occupied. But consternation—shame—horror—anguish—fury—rage—madness—all assist to delineate the scene! Who should appear but her husband! Quin was still in the room, and, perceiving Mr. L—— ready to wreak all his vengeance upon his wife, he flew to his sword and drew it in her defence. In the conflict Mr. L—— was wounded in the thigh; and this affair terminated for the present with a couple of prosecutions against Quin; the first for Crim. Con., and the next for an assault and battery.

London was now too warm a climate for our hero to respire in with safety. He flew to Dublin, where he engaged upon that theatre, and acquitted himself tolerably well in two or three parts. He learned soon after the death of Mr. L——; and his friend Ryan now prevailed upon him to return to the metropolis, and fulfil his theatrical engagements here.

CHAPTER II.

A concise view of the progress of the stage, towards its present state;
illustrated with many curious anecdotes.

In order to form a more perfect judgment of Quin's character as
an actor it will be necessary to consider the state of the stage at
that period, and take a short retrospect of its various advances
to the perfection which it has now obtained.

It is somewhat extraordinary, and deserving of observation,
though I have not met with any writer that has made the
remark, that the legal restoration of Charles II. and the restoration of the stage were events of the same period. This prince
granted two patents for the forming of two distinct companies of
comedians. That which was under the direction of Mr. Killegrew had the title of the King's Servants; and the other, under
the management of Sir William Davenant, was styled the Duke's
company. Both these companies performed at the same time,
and met with great success, having the sanction and protection
of the nobility, who now considered theatrical representations in
their true light, as the most moral and rational amusement that
can engage the vacant hours of study or business. Propriety of
action and elegance of expression had never till now been duly
attended to upon the English stage, and the present representations were moreover attended with two very critical advantages.
The first was, the theatres immediately opening after so long a
suspension of acting, during the civil war and the anarchy that
succeeded it; the second advantage was, that no woman had ever
before represented any part. The female characters had hereto-
fore been performed by the most effeminate actors in the
company.* The heightening that actresses must have at first
given to theatrical representations, when compared to the hetero-

* The managers could not, however, immediately supply all the female
characters with actresses, as we find by an anecdote that is handed down
to us by different theatrical historians, of King Charles coming a little
before his usual time to a tragedy, and finding the actors not ready to
begin, the King was impatient, and sent to know the meaning of it; when
the master of the company, coming up to the box, judging that the best
excuse for the delay would be the true one, plainly told the King that the
Queen *was not shaved yet.* At which the King laughed heartily, till the
Queen could make her appearance fresh-trimmed.

geneous appearance that the most smooth-faced comedian could have made in petticoats, is almost inconceivable. At the time that Shakespeare wrote, he was not unapprised to what a disadvantage his female characters must appear under this circumstance; and to this consideration we may reasonably attribute the scarcity with which they are strewed in most of his pieces.

The King's Servants acted then, as they do now, at the Theatre Royal in Drury Lane; and the Duke's Company at the Duke's Theatre, in Dorset Gardens. They both continued to meet with success for several years, but their managers were not yet arrived at sufficient skill in their departments; they were still ignorant how to afford the town an agreeable and constant variety; they had hitherto got up but very few stock plays, and these, by their frequent exhibition, at length satiated their audiences. Killegrew, however, who was the most skilful manager of the two, still found some resource in the superiority of his actors and the variety of their abilities; and on the other hand, Davenant, in order to balance their success, first added scenery and music to action, and introduced a theatrical medley since known by the name of Dramatic Operas. The court soon after interfered in the opposite manager's disputes, and a negociation was set on foot, which terminated in the union of their patents in the year 1864. Nevertheless, by various incidental causes, the stage languished, and was just expiring when it was again revived by King William's licence in 1695, at which period the great Betterton made his appearance, and gave the world the greatest idea they ever had of just acting upon the English stage; for we are told, and we must take the tradition of our forefathers upon these heads, that Betterton was an actor, as Shakespeare was an author, both without competitors, formed for the mntual assistance and illustration of each others' genius; that when he spoke you might see the muse of Shakespeare in her triumph, with all her beauties in her best array, rising into real life and charming her beholders.*

It would be impertinent in a modern to pretend to say

---

* "The most that a Vandyke can arrive at, is to make his portraits of great persons seem to think; a Shakespeare goes farther yet, and tells you what this picture thought; a Betterton steps beyond them both, and calls them from the grave, to breathe and be themselves again in feature, speech and motion. When the skilful actor shews you all these powers at once united, and gratifies at once your eye, your ear, and your understanding, to conceive the pleasures arising from such harmony you must have been present at it—'tis not to be told you."—*Vide* the *Apology for the Life of C. Cibber*, p. 88.

Betterton did not possess all those graces and qualities which formed the complete actor; but with due deference to our predecessors there seems such a partiality in men of the last age for everything that was then prevalent, that I cannot help suspecting either their judgment or their veracity upon many occasions, and in nothing more than with regard to actors. Cibber, in his *Apology*, says, "Had Sandford lived in Shakespeare's time, I am confident his judgment must have chose him above all other actors, to have played his Richard the Third;" and I shall only add, if Cibber, when he wrote his *Apology*, had seen Garrick in that part, he certainly would have altered his opinion.

This, perhaps, may be considered only as mere *ipse dixit*, pro and con; and it may be urged that my partiality in favour of Garrick is as strong as Cibber's might be for Betterton; but the point is surely different, when I oppose Garrick to Sandford, who, even at that time of day, was considered but as a third-rate actor, the *Spagnoles* of the theatre, the *stage-villain*, and could not be put in competition with many of our present subalterns.

But to resume: Soon after the death of Queen Mary, consort to William the Third, the theatre in Lincoln's Inn Fields, which was formed out of a tennis court, was by patent opened; when Mr. Congreve's comedy of *Love for Love* had such an extraordinary run that scarce any other play was performed till the end of the season. Mr. Congreve was then in such high esteem as an author, that besides his profits from the play, the managers offered him a whole share with them, which he accepted; in consideration of which he obliged himself to give them one new play every year. Dryden, in King Charles's time, had the same share with the King's Company, but he bound himself to give them two plays every season. This, it may be imagined, he could not long support; and it is reasonable to think he would have served them better with one a year not so hastily written. Mr. Congreve's bad state of health prevented his producing any more than one piece in the next three years, when the *Mourning Bride* made its appearance. The very first speech secured him success, and indeed, if there had not been another good line in it, what judicious critic could have condemned the production that contained these lines, especially when they were uttered by Mrs. Bracegirdle in the character of Almeria?

> Music hath charms to soothe a savage breast,
> To soften rocks, or bend a knotted oak.
> I've read that things inanimate have mov'd,
> And as with living souls have been inform'd,
> By magic numbers and persuasive sound.

> What, then, am I ?   Am I more senseless grown
> Than trees or flint !   O force of constant woe !
> 'Tis not in harmony to calm my griefs.

The next piece Mr. Congreve produced, and which was performed at the same theatre, was the comedy of *The Way of the World*, which certainly contains more sterling wit than any comedy that has been produced since. It is true, those critics who envy Congreve for his genius, aver that it is his principal defect to have too much wit, for that his very fools say good things, and all his dialogue is repartee : it is a thousand pities they could not imitate his faults ; they would greatly tend to perfect their productions. Congreve's wit, methinks, might escape uncensured without it were satiriz'd with at least as much pleasantry as the thing complained of. If, indeed, the critics had confined themselves to some of his luscious scenes, they would have had a much fairer chance of success ; but even his faults upon this score admit of some apology—the vitiated taste of the town, grounded upon the example of preceding writers. These immoralities of the stage had by avowed indulgence been creeping into it ever since the time of King Charles ; nothing that was loose could be then too low for it : the *London Cuckolds*, the most rank play that ever succeeded, was then in the highest court favour ; nor was it discountenanced till, to the honour of Mr. Garrick, he had the courage to abolish its representation on the anniversary of Lord Mayor's Day ; when the managers of the other house, whose eyes were at length opened to the propriety of the measure, followed his example.

Whilst our authors were so licentious, the ladies were observed to be decently afraid of venturing bare-faced to a new comedy, till they were assured that they might do it without the risk of insult to their modesty ; or, if their curiosity were too strong for their patience, they took care at least to save appearances, and seldom came upon the first days of acting but in mask (then daily worn, and admitted in the pit, side-boxes and gallery), which custom, however, had so many ill consequences that it has been abolished these many years. In this almost general corruption, Dryden, whose plays were famed more for their wit than their chastity, led the way, which he fairly confesses, and endeavours to excuse, in his prologue to *The Pilgrim*, revived for his Benefit in his declining age and fortune, at the beginning of this century. I shall select a few lines from this prologue to support my assertion :

> Perhaps the parson stretch'd a point too far,
> When with our theatres he waged a war.

He tells you that this very moral age
Received the first infection from the stage.
But sure a banished court, with lewdness fraught,
The seeds of open vice returning brought.
These lodg'd (as vice by great example thrives)
It first debauched their daughters and their wives.
London, a fruitful soil, yet never bore
So plentiful a crop of horns before.
The poets, who must live by courts or starve,
Were proud so good a government to serve,
And, mix'd with buffoons and with pimps profane,
Tainted the stage for some small scrap of gain.
For they, like harlots under bawds profest,
Took all the ungodly pains and got the least.
Thus did the thriving malady prevail,
The court its head, the poets but the tail;
The sin was of our native growth, 'tis true,
The scandal of the sin was wholly new.
Misses there were, but modesty concealed;
Whitehall the naked Venus first revealed;
Where, standing, as at Cyprus, in her shrine,
The strumpet was ador'd with rites divine.

Such then was the state of the stage in the beginning of this century; let us now see what farther advances it made towards decency and perfection in the course of seventeen years. As it was as yet under no particular restriction, many indecent and even libellous pieces were ushered forth, to the scandal of good manners and the insult of all civil liberty; but on the other hand, to make some amends for this, *Cato*, after being nine years sequestered in Mr. Addison's closet, made its appearance upon the public stage at the time that Booth was in his greatest perfection. The success this piece met with, as well in London as at Oxford, is beyond all comprehension, and could be surpassed by nothing but so uncommon a coalition of sentiments in the Whigs and Tories (at a time when party ran very high) who seemed emulous to surpass each other, not only in the applause they bestowed upon it, but even in the presents they made to the capital performers in it.

The Careless Husband, written by Colley Cibber, was represented at Drury Lane some time before. This comedy for the purity of the sentiment, and the justness of the characters, may be ranked foremost in the laureate's productions. He nothwithstanding, tells us that Mrs. Oldfield had a great share in its success, not only from the uncommon excellence of her action, but even from her personal manner of conversing, for, he says, there are many sentiments in the character of lady Betty Modish, that were almost originally her own, or only dressed with a little more care than when they negligently fell from her lively humour.

The principal actors at this period were, Mr. Booth, a gentleman of a liberal education, an agreeable person, and melodious voice; equally happy in his gesticulations as his elocution, and was reckoned the greatest tragedian that ever appeared on any stage—at least to those who had not seen his predecessor Betterton.   Mr. Wilks, who was a very handsome man, of a graceful mien; studious of proper attitudes and cadences, in which he excelled most of his competitors.   His forte lay in comedy, though he was no contemptible tragedian.   Mr. Doggett, the greatest original in low comedy that has ever yet appeared.   Mr. Colley Cibber, the best fop that perhaps ever performed upon any stage.   Mr. Estcourt, a great mimic, though but a middling actor. Mr. Johnson, a performer of sound judgment, who succeeded in many walks in comedy.   To whom may be added as excellent actresses, Mrs. Oldfield and Mrs. Porter; the first in comedy and the last in tragedy.

CHAPTER III.

Quin's first appearance upon the London stage; the gradual advances he
made towards speaking; the manager's opinion of his performance of
Falstaff: his uncommon success in that character. Anecdotes
concerning Ryan. An uncommon duel upon an uncommon
occasion.

MR. QUIN first made his appearance at Drury Lane in the year
1718. At that time of day, seniority of date was considered with
as much jealousy in the green-room as in the army or navy; and
an actor that should at once have rushed upon the town, with all
the powers of a Betterton or a Booth, in a capital character,
would have been looked upon by his competitors for fame as little
better than an usurper of talents and applause. Besides, the
manager considered acting as a mere mechanical acquisition,
that nothing but time could procure; and therefore, every one in
his company was to serve his apprenticeship before he attempted
being even a journeyman actor. This accounts for Quin's remaining for a long time the mere scene drudge, the faggot of the
drama. He at length, however, performed some capital parts,
and his name made its appearance in the bills (though not in
capitals) annexed to Banquo in *Macbeth*, and the Lieutenant of
the Tower in *Richard the Third*.

It was not till the year 1720, that he had an opportunity of
displaying his great theatrical powers. Upon the revival of the
Merry Wives of Windsor at Lincoln's-Inn-Fields, of which the
late Mr. Rich was the manager, there was no one in the whole
company who would undertake the part of Falstaff; Rich was,
therefore, inclined to give up all thoughts of representing it,
when Quin, happening to come in his way, said, if he pleased he
would attempt it. "Hem!" said Rich, taking a pinch of snuff,
"You attempt Falstaff!—why (hem!)—you might as well think
of acting Cato after Booth. The character of Falstaff, young
man, is quite another character from what you think" (taking
another pinch of snuff), "it is not a snivelling part, that—that—
in short, that anyone can do. There is not a man among you
that has any idea of the part but myself. It is quite out of your
walk. No, never think of Falstaff—never think of Falstaff—it
is quite—quite out of your walk, indeed, young man."

This was the reception his first effort of stepping out of the faggot walk met with, and for some days he laid aside all thoughts of ever doing Falstaff, or indeed speaking upon the stage, except it were to deliver a message. Ryan, who at that time had the ear and confidence of Rich, having heard Quin, long before he thought of coming upon the stage, repeat some passages in the character of Falstaff, prevailed upon the manager to let Quin rehearse them before him ; which he did, but not much to his master's satisfaction. However, as the case was desperate, and either the *Merry Wives of Windsor* must have been laid aside, or Quin perform Falstaff; this alternative, at length, prevailed upon Rich to admit James into the part.

The first night of his appearance in this character he surprised and astonished the audience ; no actor before ever entered into the spirit of the author, and it seemed as if Shakespeare had, by intuition, drawn the knight* so long before for Quin only to represent. The just applause he met with upon this occasion is incredible ; continued clappings and peals of laughter, in some measure interrupted the representation, though it was impossible that any regularity whatever could have more increased the mirth or excited the approbation of the audience.

It would, however, be injustice to the other performers not to acknowledge that they greatly contributed to the success of the piece, which had a very great run and was of eminent service to the company. Ryan was excellent in the part of Ford ; Spillar, reckoned among the greatest comedians of that time, performed one of his strongest parts, that of Doctor Caius ; and Boherne, another very good actor, did Justice Shallow.

Ryan, at that period, was amongst the first rate actors ; and this will not appear extraordinary, if we consider it was before the accident he met with, which occasioned his voice to falter, as we may remember in our own time, that he was very genteel in his person, was elegant in his action, and was always correct in his part. The accident here mentioned was : Going home one night alone from the play-house, he was attacked by two street robbers near Lincoln's-Inn-Fields, when Ryan drew his sword in his defence and one of the villains fired a pistol at him, which lodged a ball in his throat. It was extracted by a very eminent surgeon while it was a matter of debate with the faculty whether

---

* *Henry the Fourth* was, at the same time, performed at Drury Lane Theatre, where Booth did Hotspur ; Wilks, the Prince of Wales ; Cibber, Glendour ; and Harper, Sir John Falstaff. Nothwithstanding three of the parts were so well cast and Harper was no bad comedian, and a figure of the knight, this play did not meet with any applause, in comparison to what it did in Lincoln's-Inn-Fields, which was entirely owing to Quin's doing Falstaff.

the wound was mortal.   It proved otherwise, but it greatly affected his voice to the end of his life.   This accident, however, never diminished his salary, and to the last hour he continued receiving as much as he had done in the greatest zenith of his acting ; so permanent and inviolable a friendship did there exist between Mr. Rich and Ryan, and the latter never once deserted him in all the various revolutions of the stage.

These remarks are perhaps somewhat antedated, but as I may not have another fair opportunity of mentioning Ryan again as an actor, I hope to be excused inserting them here, rather than drag them in head and shoulders in another place.

Soon after Quin came upon the stage, a duel was fought in Hyde Park for an actress ; the only duel upon record, that ever was fought for an actress ; but this is not astonishing when it is known that it was for no less a personage than the (afterwards) celebrated Polly Peachum—she who could captivate the great and intrepid soul of Captain Macheath, and vanquish the pride and honour of the D—— of B——, who entitled her to figure to the end of her days as a D——.

She was in the upper boxes at the representation of a new performance, when a gentleman of the army, who was sat next to her, said some civil things to her, which her theatrical virtue construed into an insult and the son of Mars had the mortification to find that all his *soft things* were thrown away upon her. The next time she appeared upon the st e, the Captain happened to come somewhat surcharged with cla , and recollecting the lady's insolence a few evenings before, began to give her a serenade of cat-calls which interrupted the play.

A *man of fashion*, who sat next to the Captain and had the lady's glory at heart, told him " He behaved very ill, and ought to be turned out." This was sufficient, they retired to an adjacent tavern in order to settle their difference in an amicable way, and cut one another's throats, whilst the tragedy went peaceably on, without any uproar or bloodshed.   But the *man of fashion* having more prudence than to contend with anyone in his profession, he declined fighting with swords, but agreed meeting the next morning in Hyde Park to decide the affair with pistols. They met accordingly, and the *man of fashion* was *à-la-mode de l'honneur*, mortally wounded in the skirt of his coat.

CHAPTER IV.

Curious and entertaining anecdotes of the theatre. The origin of their
being guarded by the military power. A few strictures thereupon,
and its effect illustrated. Quin's extraordinary fortitude and
presence of mind in a capital character: an unlucky adventure,
which costs him his liberty and endangers his life.

THE theatres till now had never been guarded by any but civil
officers, when a riot that happened in the year 1721 at the theatre
in Lincoln's Inn Fields, gave occasion to the military power
being added to the civil, for the protection of the audience, as
well as the players, from insult. As this is a memorable epoch
in dramatic history, the reader will, doubtless, not be displeased
to meet with the anecdote that gave rise to this extraordinary
measure.

A certain noble earl, who was said (and with some degree of
certainty, as he drank usquebaugh constantly at his waking) to
have been in a state of intoxication for six years, was behind
the scenes at the close of a comedy, and, seeing one of his companions on the other side among the performers, crossed the
stage, and was accordingly hissed by the audience. Mr. Rich
was on the side the noble earl came over to, and on hearing the
uproar in the house at such an irregularity, the manager said,
"I hope your lordship will not take it ill if I give orders to the
stage door keeper not to admit you any more." On his saying
that his lordship saluted Mr. Rich with a slap on the face, which
he immediately returned, and, his lordship's face being round
and fat, made his cheek ring with the force of it. Upon this
spirited return my lord's drunken companions collected themselves
directly, and Mr. Rich was to be put to death ; but Quin, Ryan,
Walker, &c., &c., stood forth in the defence of the manager, and
a grand scuffle ensued, by which the gentlemen were all drove
out at the stage door into the street. They then sallied into the
boxes, with their swords drawn, and broke the sconces, cut the
hangings, which were gilt leather, finely painted, and continued
the riot until Mr. Quin came round with a constable and watch-
men, and charged them every one into custody. They were
carried before Justice Hungerford, who then lived in the neigh-
bourhood, and all bound over to answer the consequences; but
they were soon persuaded by their wiser friends to make up this

matter, and the manager got ample redress. The King, being informed of the whole affair, was highly offended, and ordered a guard to attend that theatre as well as the other; which is continued to this day.*

No doubt it was the opinion of the managers, and some other people at that time, that the appearance of the military power at the theatre would suppress all future disturbances there, and that none would be so fool-hardy as to oppose cat calls and pippins to fusees and bayonets; but it was not considered how far the soldiers had a power to act on these occasions, or if they had once attempted to avail themselves of the superiority of their arms, whether this would not immediately have been construed into dragooning the town into the approbation of a new piece or a new actor, or whether a single bayonet being used, or a single musket being fired, would not have been more fatal to the managers, than the tearing up of all the benches in pit and gallery. Critics alone would not have stood forth champions in the cause of dramatic liberty; the political and ministerial writers of the times, and many there were at that period, would doubtless have taken the cue, and represented this among the various evils arising from standing armies. The administration at that time were certainly of this opinion, and therefore though they granted the managers the apparent assistance of military aid, as many paper soldiers, or their own scene-shifting guards would have been of equal service to them in any time of real emergency.

Experience has since repeatedly evinced the truth of these observations. Scarce had the managers fortified their theatrical garrisons before they were obliged to surrender at discretion to an unarmed few. A new pantomime was brought out at Drury Lane Theatre, which was to end with a grand dance; Madam Chateauneuf, the head dancer at that time was to have been the principal performer; but she being taken ill, the dance was necessarily set aside, though the managers published her name three successive nights, without making any apology for the omission. The first night the audience remained pretty quiet; the second they only hissed; but on the third night they ushered out the ladies, and then began to demolish the house. The first motion that was made, and by a noble marquis, was to fire it, but that being carried in the negative, they began with the orchestra, broke the harpsichord and bass viols, together with the looking glasses, scenes and chandeliers; pulled up the benches in the pit, broke down the boxes, and even the royal arms. It is true, the

* See Victor's *History of the Theatres.*

noble lord who was the ringleader, relenting the next day, in his cooler moments, of this outrage, sent a bank note of a hundred pounds to the manager; but this was a very small reparation of the damage sustained. Upon this occasion the guards remained neuter.

Another tumult happened at the same theatre a very short time after, on account of the managers continuing raised prices to old entertainments, but this conflict ended without any *bloodshed*, or even *scene slaughter*. After two or three nights' disturbance, a country gentleman was taken out of the upper boxes (the civil power only acting) and carried before Justice Deveil, but as usual his worship declined going through with his theatrical part. This unwarrantable step (though, perhaps, the constables might have acted by virtue of warrants) irritated the audience so much that they insisted upon Mr. Fleetwood's coming upon the stage; but as he was not an actor, he pleaded the privilege of being exempted from appearing on the public stage; but sent them word, that he was ready to confer with any number that should be deputed to meet him in the green-room. The representatives of the audience were accordingly chosen, and so completely executed their commission, as to obtain of the manager all they requested.

But the most general opposition to theatrical measures was upon another occasion, at the Little Theatre in the Haymarket; and as this affair merits more serious attention than either of the former, the reader will, doubtless, not be displeased to meet with a few previous reflections, which it is hoped will not appear impertinent.

The French tongue had, by the artifice of Louis the Fourteenth's administration, been industriously promulgated throughout Europe; it was spoken at all the courts, and bid fair to be the universal language; a necessary step, according to the opinion of that all-grasping prince, towards universal empire. To this end comedians were trained up in France, and at convenient times dispersed throughout the capital cities of Europe; and this was thought a favourable juncture for them to make their appearance at London. The proprietors of the Little Theatre in the Haymarket were so infatuated as to imagine French comedies would amuse and instruct the town, and absolutely introduced them upon that stage. But the public took the alarm, and even resolved to suppress the insult, as every true Englishman then considered it. The curtain drew up with the actors surrounded by guards, well knowing they stood in need of much protection; but this step no way intimidated the audience, who, being resolved not to let them go on, began regularly with cat calls, then a volley of pippins, and thirdly a general discharge of rotten eggs. The proprietors were now terrified, more especially when they found the soldiers remain motionless, and quaking behind the scenes at the consequences; at length, as their last resource, they sent for Justice Deveil to read the Riot Act. But Sir Thomas, so far from being allowed to proceed in this business, found himself under the absolute necessity of ordering with his own voice both troops and actors off the stage. The warriors and comedians being now retired, the audience thought it was time to testify their resentment to the proprietors for their impudent and insolent attempt, and accordingly demolished without reserve all the benches, scenes, and decorations. Nor did the ambassadors of France and Spain, who were present upon this occasion, escape with impunity, but had a share of abuse to divide between them proportioned to their rank, and which they were compelled to hear, as they could not get away; the cutting of the traces of their carriages having been judged a very proper preliminary step to make sure of the honour of their company during this whole comi-tragi-farcical conflict.

The spirit which was shewn against the French comedians engendered many tumults, which the undiscerning multitude imagined equally popular and national as the opposition to Gallic performers and performances. This contagion spread from the Haymarket to Drury Lane, and furnished Quin with many opportunities of testifying his natural prowess, as well as his jocular persuasive abilities, which frequently succeeded. He has more than once appeased an audience by telling them a story, when they were elevated to the highest pitch of rage at the play not beginning in time. His famous story of *the round and square trenchers* is well known, and it is equally well testified that he absolutely told this story to a crowded house, one night when the play could not begin till the arrival of some of the royal family, who did not come till past seven.

The following anecdote is also related of him, but with what degree of truth the editor of these sheets will not pretend to determine. There was one evening a riot at the stage door, when Mr. Quin wounded a young fellow, who had drawn upon him, slightly in the hand. The spark presently after came into one of the green boxes over the stage door. The play was *Macbeth*, and in the fine soliloquy where he sees the imaginary dagger, as Quin repeated,

"And on thy blade are drops of reeking blood,"

the young fellow bawled out, "Ay—reeking indeed! What,

does your conscience prick you ? You rascal, that's my blood you drew just now." Quin, giving him a severe side-look, replied just loud enough to be heard by him, "Damn your blood, I say," and then without the least hesitation went on with the speech; so that the major part of the audience scarce noticed the interruption. The only comment that shall be made upon this story is, that if it be true it was a proof of a most extraordinary presence of mind, vast coolness of temper, and uncommon fortitude; no small qualifications to perfect an actor; for not to be visibly flustered at any little interruption which he may meet with whilst upon the stage, or in the course of his speech, is one of those negative qualifications that may be put in competition with the more brilliant excellencies of capital performers. How few actors there are who, in similar circumstances, would not have deprived the audience of a material share of their entertainment, in one of the most principal scenes, the reader is left to determine from his own knowledge and experience.

I am sorry to find myself brought to that period of Mr. Quin's life which is equally disagreeable to recollect as it is to recite.

Every one who knew Mr. Quin whilst upon the stage must have been sensible that notwithstanding the rough fantastic manner which so much characterized him, no one was of a more humane disposition, or less addicted to revenge : this may be gathered from his behaviour upon various occasions, and particularly to the self-sufficient Theophilus Cibber. There was at this time upon Drury Lane Theatre a subaltern player, or rather faggot, whose name never made its appearance in the bills, and therefore will scarce be found in the annals of the theatres of that period : Williams, however, was the name he bore; he was a native of Wales, and was not the least nettlesome of his countrymen. He performed the part of the Messenger in the tragedy of *Cato*, and in saying "Cæsar sends health to Cato," he pronounced the last word *Keeto*; which so struck Quin that he replied, with his usual coolness, "Would he had sent a better messenger." This reply so stung Mr. Williams that he from that moment vowed revenge : he followed Quin into the green room when he came off the stage, and after representing the injury he had done him by making him appear ridiculous in the eyes of the audience, and thereby hurting him in his profession, he then called him to an account as a gentleman, and insisted upon satisfaction. But Quin, with his usual philosophy and humour, endeavoured to rally his passion. This did but add fuel to his antagonist's rage, who, without further remonstrance, retired, and waited for Quin under the Piazza, upon his return from the tavern to his lodging. Williams drew upon him, and a rencounter ensued, in which Williams fell.

Quin was tried for this affair at the Old Bailey, and it was brought in manslaughter, to the entire satisfaction of the court and all who were acquainted with the origin and progress of this quarrel.

CHAPTER V.

The state of the theatre at the time of the *Beggar's Opera* coming out; its
success.　The fate of Cibber's attempt in the same way, and of the
second part of Mr. Gay's opera.　The origin of the licensing act;
to whom we are indebted for it.　Mr. Quin's further progress
as an actor; engages at Drury Lane; the revolutions of
that theatre; the uncommon applause he meets with
in the character of Cato.

NOTWITHSTANDING Quin's great merit, added to the abilities of
Ryan, Boherne, Spillar, Griffin, Egleton, and the two Bullocks,
who were at that time considered as actors of the first class in
their different walks, Booth and Wilks had so far the ascendency
over the taste and judgment of the town that they carried all
before them; and from the time of the run of the *Merry Wives
of Windsor* Rich could never fill his house without orders, till he
introduced pantomimes, and acted Harlequin himself; or rather,
till he, with much reluctance, was prevailed upon to perform
Gay's *Beggar's Opera*, which came out in 1727, and had such
amazing success.　*Cato*, it is true, met with great applause, but
this opera had a run of forty nights longer than that much-
admired tragedy.

This uncommon reception of the *Beggar's Opera* induced Colley
Cibber to attempt something of the same kind next year, under
the title of *Love in a Riddle*; but how different was its reception
from Gay's production! it was damned to the lowest regions of
infamy the very first night, which so mortified Cibber, that it
threw him into a fever; and from this moment he resolved, as
soon as he conveniently could, to leave the stage, and no longer
submit himself or his talents to the capricious taste of the town.

It was then generally thought that his jealousy of Gay, and
the high opinion he entertained of his new piece, had operated
so strongly, as to make him set every engine in motion to get the
sequel of the *Beggar's Opera*, called *Polly*, suppressed, in order to
engross the town entirely to *Love in a Riddle*.　Whether Cibber
did or did not bestir himself in this affair, it is certain that Gay
and Rich had the mortification to see all their hopes of a succeeding harvest blasted, by the Lord Chamberlain's absolute
prohibition of it, after it had been rehearsed and was just ready
to bring out.

This naturally leads me to say a few words upon the origin

and intent of the licensing act. Colley Cibber tells us that a broken wit collected a fourth company, who for some time acted plays in the Haymarket, which house the united Drury Lane comedians had quitted. This enterprizing person (Henry F——d——g) had sense enough to know that the best plays with bad actors would turn but to a very poor account; and therefore thought it necessary to give the public some pieces of an extraordinary kind, the poetry of which he conceived ought to be so strong, that the greatest dunce of an actor could not spoil it. He knew too, that as he was in haste to get money, it would take up less time to be intrepidly abusive, than decently entertaining; that to draw the mob after him, he must rake the channel, and pelt their superiors; that to shew himself somebody, he must come up to Juvenal's advice and stand the consequence. Such then was the nettlesome modesty he set out with; upon this principle he produced several frank and free farces, that seemed to knock all distinctions of mankind on the head. Religion, laws, government, priests, judges, and ministers, were all laid flat at the feet of this Herculean satyrist, this Drawcansir in wit, that spared neither friend nor foe; who to make his fame immortal, like another Erostratus, set fire to his stage, by writing up to an act of parliament to demolish it.

The most remarkable of these politico-satyrical pieces were *Pasquin, The Historical Register*, and *Eurydice Hissed*; but he did not confine himself solely to stage abuse; for about the same time he attacked Sir Robert W——e in a most violent manner in the paper called *The Champion*, written as the title sets forth, by Hercules Vinegar; and doubtless the laureate obliquely hints at this title, when he calls him the *Herculean satyrist*.

To Henry F——d——g then are we indebted for the licensing act, and the theatrical power that is now lodged in the licenser; who exercised his authority for the first time in 1730, upon *Gustavus Vasa*, a tragedy written by Mr. Brooke. Whether it has been productive of some good or evil in its consequences, is a disquisition that would lead me too far out of my way; but such readers as choose to enter more largely upon this subject, are referred to the periodical productions of that time, wherein they will find it most elaborately discussed.

The next capital character that Quin appeared in at Lincoln's-Inn-Fields (where the general applause he now met with, compelled the manager to think that he might have some small merit in Sir John Falstaff) was that of Sir John Brute in the *Provoked Wife*. This play which was written by Sir John Vanbrugh was revived at Drury-lane about the year 1725, after having been laid aside for some years on account of its immoral tendency. Many

of the most offensive parts were now omitted, and the whole
night scene where Sir John Brute appears in women's apparel,
was substituted for one wherein the Knight represented an in-
ebriate parson, and as such a professed debauchee.

Soon after the revival of this play at Drury Lane, many un-
avoidable accidents, and none more than the bad reception
Cibber's *Love in a Riddle* met with, brought on the dissolution of
that company. Booth's ill state of health prevented him for
some time before his death appearing on the stage. Mrs. Oldfield's
death, which happened in the year 1730, deprived the theatre of
one of its greatest ornaments. Mrs. Porter was about the same
time lost to the stage, by the dislocation of her leg ; and the death
of Wilks in the year 1731, gave the finishing stroke to this
declining company.

It is now that we may expect to find Mr. Quin shine forth in
all his splendour, having no longer those powerful competitors
and favourites of the town, Booth and Wilks, to contend with.

The run of the *Beggar's Opera*, about the time of the revival
of the *Provoked Wife* at Lincoln's-Inn-Fields, prompted Quin to
leave that theatre, where his talents lay dormant, as he could
neither perform the part of Macheath, nor that still more
illustrious one of Harlequin, which the manager considered as a
more capital part than Hamlet or Cato, and therefore kept it
entirely to himself ; and to do him justice, it must be acknowledged he was very great in this particular *walk*.

When Quin first engaged at Drury-lane, he succeeded the elder
Mills in all the capital parts of tragedy, and Delane supplied his
place at Lincoln's-Inn-Fields, after having performed for some
time with tolerable success at Goodman's Fields. But it was
upon Booth's quitting the stage, on account of his illness, that
Quin shone forth in all his splendour; and yet he had the diffidence
upon the first night of his appearing in *Cato*, to insert in the bills,
that *the part of Cato would be only attempted by Mr. Quin.*
The modesty of this invitation produced a full house, and a
favourable audience, but the actor's own peculiar merit effected
more. When he came to that part of the play where his dead
son is brought upon the bier, Quin, in speaking these words,

" Thanks to the Gods !—my boy has done his duty,"

so affected the whole house that they cried out with a continued
acclamation, " Booth outdone !   Booth outdone !"

Yet this was not the summit of his applause; for when he
repeated the famous soliloquy he was *encored* to that degree,
that, though it was submitting to an impropriety, he indulged
the audience with its repetition.

CHAPTER VI.

Theatrical revolutions during Mr. Quin's holding the first rank upon the
stage. Anecdotes of managers and actors, which set the dramatic
transactions of those times in a clear point of view. Theophilus
Cibber's treachery to his master, and Quin's treatment of
him. An adventure between our hero and a poet.

WE now see Mr. Quin arrived at the summit of his profession,
where he remained without a rival for full ten years.   But,
though he was in quiet possession of the first rank upon the
stage, the stage itself did not continue in this peaceable state all
this while. Various were the fermentations and revolutions of
the theatre during the course of this period, some of the most
remarkable of which I shall take notice of, as Mr. Quin's interest
and character were very immediately connected with them.

The tyranny of the managers of Drury Lane house, to whom
Booth and Cibber sold their shares, was so great that it was
unanimously agreed by the whole company to desert their
masters, and set up for themselves in the Little Theatre in the
Haymarket, which they accordingly did in 1733.   The managers,
who were highly irritated at this proceeding, were advised to put
the act of the twenty-first of Queen Anne in force against the
deserted heroes.   Sir Thomas Deveil, who was always a very
active, though not a very successful, magistrate in all theatrical
altercations, granted a warrant, by virtue whereof one of the
chief performers was taken upon the stage, while he was
performing, and committed to Bridewell : but he was discharged,
as he was not within the meaning of the act, being a housekeeper,
and having a vote for the representatives of the city of West-
minster in parliament.

This unexpected triumph operated so strongly upon the Drury
Lane managers, that Highmore and his confederates had no
thoughts but of abdicating their thrones, which they proposed
doing, however, only to the best bidder.   And yet if these
gentlemen patentees had either been acquainted with the real
situation of their revolted actors' affairs, or had been possessed of
fortitude enough to have undertaken another campaign, the
deserters must have surrendered at discretion.

The manager of the other house had probably been let into the secret, or gained such intelligence as made him think the Drury Lane patent a desirable acquisition. He accordingly framed the project of becoming the manager of both houses—what a torrent of pantomimes would the town have been deluged with! and what a comfortable situation would the best actors have been in, had this scheme taken place, when they would have had no other master to have flown to for redress and encouragement! The reason that this design proved abortive was that it could not be carried into execution by Rich alone, as he was deficient in the most material point—the *res pecuniaria*. He therefore made application to his friend Mr. Fleetwood, and proposed to him that he should purchase the patent in his name, as well to secure to him the property he should disburse, as to save appearances with the town, who would perhaps become jealous of what might be construed into a monopoly in Rich, and that he would pay Fleetwood at fixed periods such sums as would entitle him to a moiety of the profits as arising from Drury Lane.

When this project got wind, the actors in the Haymarket were in the utmost consternation lest it should succeed; as they would have been compelled to submit to whatever conditions he might have imposed, so calamitous was the state of their affairs, which became every day more desperate.

At this critical juncture a misunderstanding arose between Fleetwood and Rich; so that the first, who became a purchaser of five-sixths of the shares of Drury Lane house, broke off all connexion with Rich, and remained sole manager of that theatre. This was a favourable incident to the mutineers, who had a *carte blanche* offered them from Fleetwood, and they accordingly disposed of their scenes and wardrobe to him, and 'listed under his banner, with better salaries than were ever before paid any company. The general conditions were, two hundred pounds a year to each managing actor, and a clear benefit. Quin was engaged at the same time by Fleetwood, but upon still more advantageous terms, and such, indeed, as no hired actor ever had before. This was proof that he was now at the summit of his profession, and that he had no competitor either for recompense or applause.

Notwithstanding Theophilus Cibber was amongst the foremost of the mutineers who found protection under Mr. Fleetwood's banner, of so ungrateful a cast was the progeny of the laureate that, when Mr. Fleetwood was confined by a fit of the gout, he circulated reports that his affairs were in so bad a situation, and he was in such great arrears with his actors, that though he might recover from his indisposition there was no likelihood of his ever returning to the management of the stage; nay, he prevailed upon his father to exert his influence with the L—d C———n, in order to obtain a licence for another playhouse, as Mr. Fleetwood had very injuriously treated his principal actors. These reports, which were the offspring of The.'s brain, had just the effect which every honest man would desire. It was upon this occasion that some opprobrious words passed between Quin and Cibber, who denied his having had any hand in the propagation of these calumnies. Quin, who had always looked upon him as an impertinent coxcomb, had now as much reason to abhor as he had before to despise him, and when The. talked about satisfaction in a gentlemanlike manner, Quin said with a laugh, " Quarrelling with such a fellow is like———" (using an indecent expression), and walked off as cool as if nothing had happened. This was more cutting to The. than if he had said the severest sarcasm that could have been uttered. He never forgave Quin for it, but merely on this account abuses him upon every occasion in what he calls an *Apology for his Life*, which is one of the most trifling, insignificant productions that was ever put together; for it cannot be said to be written, as everything that is worth reading in it is stolen from his father's *Apology*. This was also the source of that quarrel which afterwards ended in a duel and a flight at the Bedford coffee house, and which will be found in the sequel of this Life.

When Cibber had thus thrown himself out of Fleetwood's confidence, Quin supplied his place in presiding over rehearsals, and the perusal of such new plays as were offered.

There is a story told of him, concerning his behaviour to an author upon one of these occasions, which carries with it a good deal the air of truth. A poet had put a tragedy which he had just finished, into his hands one night behind the scenes, whilst he was still dressed for the character he had performed. Quin put it into his pocket, and never thought any more about it: the bard who was very impatient to know his sentiments with regard to the piece, waited upon him one morning, in order to hear his doom. Quin gave some reasons for its not being proper for the stage, after having learned the title and the fable, which he was before entirely unacquainted with: upon which the poet, whose muse had flattered him with the perspective view of a new suit of clothes, as well as the clearing the chandler's shop score, in a faltering voice desired to have his piece returned. "There," said Quin, "it lies in the window." Upon which poor Bayes repaired to the window and took up a play which proved to be a comedy, and his muse had brought forth a direful tragedy;

whereupon he told Quin of the mistake;—who very pleasantly said, "Faith, then, Sir, I have certainly lost your play." "*Lost my play!*" cries the poet, almost thunderstruck. "Yes, by —— but I have," replied Quin,—"but look ye, here is a drawer full of both comedies and tragedies—take any two you will in the room of it." But this in no way satisfied the poet, who imagined that no one's Pegasus had so luxuriant a district to graze on as his own upon the common of Parnassus. "My play or a benefit; if not, sir, I shall commence a prosecution against you and the manager." Such were the terms of the bard:—he had the run of the house, and was completely satisfied; being fully persuaded that his next production (which, by-the-bye, was the identical same in a rough copy) would not fail of being performed.

CHAPTER VII.

The difficult task of managers, particularly with regard to writers; the
manner in which the different managers of this century have behaved
upon these occasions. The genteel method Mr. Garrick pursues.
An author's disgrace upon the second night of the representation of his piece. The duty of a manager according
to the poet laureate.

THE story related of Mr. Quin, in the last chapter, when he was
deputy manager of Drury Lane house, naturally leads to some reflections upon the embarrassments the masters of playhouses most
frequently meet with upon these occasions.

If a manager refuses a play by saying "that he has so many
pieces to bring on this season that he would not amuse the
gentleman with hopes to his prejudice, while, perhaps, the
manager of the other house would be very glad of the performance," he is looked upon as a stupid, ignorant coxcomb, to say
anything of a play before he has seen it; or that if ignorance is
not the ground-work of his behaviour, partiality must be so; or
else he may be giving the preference to contemptible works,
whilst he refuses to accept of those that may be of great worth
and excellence. If, like Wilkes, when he was one of the patentees,
he should pay the author compliments on his piece that it did not
deserve, and omit mentioning such beauties as might have escaped
him, none but a fool could be pleased, and such could never be
the author of a work of this nature, and as a man of sense he
must hold the manager's judgment in the highest contempt. If,
like the laureate, he returned a poet his play with saying "That
it was not fit for the stage," an author might pertinently reply
"If, Sir, in other respects it is a good piece, it may be easily
rendered theatrical, as this is a mechanical quality and is like the
jeu de theatre to an actor;—it can never confer merit, but may
hide defects." If, like the late Mr. Rich, whose judgments were
always particularly *laconic*, he should communicate his answer as
this manager constantly did, in the same identical four words,—
"It will not do;"—an author might perhaps shrewdly add,—"for
you—who form the same opinion upon all works except pantomimes." Or if, indeed, like Mr. Fleetwood, who piqued himself
upon being the gentleman, more particularly on these occasions,
as he had *gentlemen only* to deal with, he should avoid as long as

c

possible giving the mortifying refusal, and at length after having
perhaps driven the poor poet to his last shirt, acquit himself in the
most polite terms possible ; a hungry author would certainly damn
him for a fawning equivocating scoundrel, and for the next toast,
in small beer give "More beef, and less complaisance." But if,
like a certain manager, who has presided for almost twenty years
over the best regulated company of comedians in Europe, he
should, when a play is offered to him, read it with attention, be
always accessible to the author and diligent in giving a fair and
candid opinion of the piece without equivocation or disguise, and
such an opinion as would constantly stand the test of sound
criticism ; no one but the vain, self-sufficient, disappointed
poetaster would ever be offended at a similar conduct, and even
such a contemptible animal as this, must not be so callous to all
literary fame, as not to be better pleased with a genteel representation of his errors and inability, than to be damned the first
night of his piece's representation, to the lowest regions of public
infamy.

I shall illustrate this observation with a genuine anecdote. In
the reign of Queen Anne, a solemn bard, who, like Bayes in the
Rehearsal, wrote only for fame and reputation, upon the second
day's public triumph of his muse, marching in a stately full
bottomed peruke into the lobby of the house with a lady of con-
dition in his hand, and raising his voice to the Sir Fopling sound,
that became the mouth of a man of quality, and calling out—
"Hey, box-keeper, where is my lady such a one's servant?" was
unfortunately answered by honest John Trott, (which then
happened to be the box-keeper's real name) "Sir, we are dis-
missed ; there was not company enough to pay candles." In
which mortal astonishment it may be sufficient to leave him,
exclaiming against the barbarous taste of the age, their want of
judgment, and the like.

But the difficulties and embarrassments which managers labour
under, are not confined merely to poets ; they have many refractory subjects in their commonwealth—many turbulent spirits
in their state, who are constantly raising commotions ; the
progress of which nothing but the most vigilant attention,
animating the utmost latitude of human prudence, can frequently
prevent. And therefore if when they have gained the public
esteem, by affording the town a rational and variegated amusement, they may be supposed to be handsomely rewarded for their
pains, it is no more than what they most laboriously earn. No
reasonable man ever grudged a lord chancellor his income, and if
small things may be compared with great, by a parity of reasoning,

no generous man should covet the much inferior profits of the far
more laborious and embarrassing task of a theatrical manager.
Perhaps the reader may not be thoroughly acquainted with the
vocations of a dramatic governor and therefore I shall give him
a short sketch of them, as Colley Cibber represented them to the
court of King's Bench when he was counsel in his own cause de-
pending with Sir Richard Steele.

THE DUTY OF A MANAGER.

" By our books it is apparent, that the managers have under
their care no less than a hundred and forty persons in constant
daily pay; and among such numbers, it will be no wonder, if a
great number of them are unskilful, and sometimes untractable,
all which tempers are to be led or driven, watched and restrained,
by the continual skill, care and patience of the managers. Every
manager is obliged in his turn to attend two or three times every
morning at the rehearsal of plays and other entertainments for the
stage, or else every rehearsal would be but a rude meeting of
mirth and jollity. The same attendance is as necessary at every
play, during the time of its public action, in which one or more
of us have constantly been punctual, whether we have any part
in the play or not. A manager ought to be at the reading of
every new play when it is at first offered to the stage, though
there is seldom one of those plays in twenty, which, upon hearing,
proves to be fit for it; and upon such occasions the attendance
must be allowed to be as painfully tedious, as the getting rid of
the authors of such plays must be disagreeable and difficult.
Besides this, a manager is to order all new clothes, to assist in
the fancy and propriety of them, to limit the expense and to
withstand the unreasonable importunities of some, who are apt
to think themselves injured, if they are not finer than their
fellows. A manager is to direct and oversee the painters,
machinists, musicians, singers and dancers, to have an eye upon
the doorkeepers, under servants and officers, who, without such
care, are too often apt to defraud us, or neglect their duty."

Such are the outlines of the duty of a manager, which must
appear no very easy employment to fill with propriety, as it
necessarily requires a thorough knowledge of all the things that
relate to the stage and its decorations, and an uncommon share of
sense and foresight, to apply them to the most advantage. I
shall make no farther comment upon this business, which, perhaps,
to some of my readers, may be considered as a tedious digression,
though so immediately connected with the person and subject I
am writing upon.

CHAPTER VIII.

A view of the stage at the time of Mr. Garrick's first appearance. His
superior abilities impartially represented.

WE now approach that period, when the great theatrical
luminary, who has shone with such transcendent splendour
for five and twenty years, first made his appearance upon our
horizon. Let us for a moment view the state of the stage at this
crisis, and the principal actors whom he so far and suddenly
eclipsed, that their names were scarce ever after mentioned but
as mere theatrical satellites. We must however exclude from
this number our buskined hero, though it must at the same time
be acknowledged, that he lost his rank in many parts that he
before performed without a rival.

Quin was at that time at the head of the Drury-lane company,
and had not met with any sort of competitor since the death of
Booth, till Delane having gained the ascendant at Covent-garden,
had some blind admirers, who put him upon an equal footing with
Quin, of whom he was little more than the copy; and even in
those very points which the nicer judges condemned him for,
particularly a monotony, which the critics called languid; but
this defect Quin could emerge from whenever he chose to exert
himself, which he was the more assiduous in now doing, as even
his petty rivalship created an emulation in him to distinguish
his superiority. On the other hand Quin's solemn sameness of
pronunciation, which communicated so much dignity to the part
of Cato, could never be imitated by Delane: add to this, that
Quin's action was always elegant, and suited to the character he
appeared in; whereas Delane's was seldom or never so. In a
word though the prejudiced, or ill judges might rank Delane in
the same class as Quin, the town, whose opinion seldom errs in
this respect, by a great majority pronounced our hero still
unrivalled.

These then were the two principal actors, at the time that Mr.
Garrick made his first appearance in the character of Richard the
Third at Goodman's Fields in the year 1740-1 when that theatre
was under the management of Mr. Gifford. He displayed at the
very earliest dawn a somewhat more than meridian brightness;
his excellence dazzled and astonished everyone; and the seeing a

young man, in no more than his twenty-fourth year, and a novice
to the stage, reaching at one single step that height of perfection,
which maturity of years and long practical experience had not
been able to bestow on the then capital performers of the English
stage, was a phenomenon, which could not but become the object
of universal speculation and as universal admiration. Quin was
the only actor that could be opposed to him in any particular
character; but it was soon manifested that Garrick's universality,
by reason of his natural endowments and acquired accomplish-
ments, would no longer admit of any competitor for theatrical
fame: for Mr. Garrick though low in his person, is well shaped
and neatly proportioned, and having added the qualifications of
dancing and fencing to that natural gentility of manner which no
art can bestow, but which our great mother nature endows many
with from infancy; his deportment is constantly easy, natural
and engaging; his complexion is dark, and the features of his
face are pleasingly regular, and animated by a full black eye,
brilliant and penetrating: his voice is clear, melodious and com-
manding, and although it may not possess the strong over-bearing
powers of Mossop's, or the musical sweetness of Barry's, yet it
appears to have a much greater compass of variety than either;
and from Mr. Garrick's judicious manner of conducting it, enjoys
that articulation and piercing distinctness, which renders it
equally intelligible, even to the most distant parts of an audience,
in the gentle whispers of murmuring love, the half smothered
accents of in-felt passion, or the professed and sometimes awkward
concealments of a side speech in comedy, as in the rants of rage,
the darings of despair or the open violence of tragical enthusiasm.

Such are the outlines of a picture, that is completely original,
whose every feature bears the stamp of nature; for it is from her
alone, that this great performer has taken all his lessons; and as
she is in herself inexhaustible, it is not surprising that her
darling son should find an unlimited scope for change and di-
versity. To what else can we attribute those innumerable
variations of passion which he can so promptly express? Rage
and ridicule, doubt and despair, transport and tenderness, com-
passion and contempt, love, jealousy, fear, fury and simplicity;
these and many more that want a name, all in turn take
possession of his features, while each in turn appears to be the
sole possessor of those features. One night old age sits on his
countenance, as if the wrinkles she had stamped were indelible;
the next, the gaiety and bloom of youth seem to overspread his
face, and smoothe even those marks, which time and muscular
conformation may have really made there. Of these truths no

one can be ignorant, who has ever seen him in the several characters of Lear, or Hamlet, Richard, Dorilas, Romeo, or Lusignan; in his Ranger, Bayes, Drugget, Kitely or Benedick. In a word, there never existed any one performer, that came near his excellence in so great a variety of opposite characters.

And now I have done this justice to Mr. Garrick's singular merit, let it be at the same time remembered, that Quin was still by far the best Sir John Brute, our only Cato, and remained quite unrivalled in Sir John Falstaff. And indeed, Quin had still many partisans who would not allow Garrick to be his superior in any tragic character; but as prejudice and partiality, doubtless then prompted them to support this opinion, it would be ridiculous *now* to maintain it, when even these very sticklers for Quin have long since been convinced of their error; and if they have not publicly recanted, they have been actuated more by pride than candour.

CHAPTER IX.

The dramatic characters of Mr. Barry, Mrs. Cibber, Mrs. Woffington, Mrs. Pritchard, and Mrs. Clive. Strictures upon Mr. Quin's indelicacy to the ladies; and an apology for suppressing the relation of part of his amours.

ABOUT the year 1745, Mr. Quin was obliged, by the vicissitudes of Mr. Fleetwood's affairs, to quit Drury Lane theatre, and engaged once more with Mr. Rich at Covent Garden. It is almost needless to repeat here, that Mr. Garrick and Mr. Quin were considered as the two capital actors till Mr. Barry made his appearance upon the English Stage; but his walk was so entirely confined to tragedy, that he did not seem to be a competitor with either of them, but in some particular parts, which were of the more tender cast, and which was a province that Mr. Quin had never attempted. It must be acknowledged, however, that Mr. Barry's success in the parts of Romeo and Castalio, entitled him to a rank with either of them ; and that, in the opinion of many, he surpassed even Mr. Garrick in these characters, though he fell far short of him in all others. A fine figure, with a most harmonious voice, added to a great command of expressive features, gave him that ascendancy in the lover's part which few beside him could ever claim.

It would be injurious to the memory of the actresses of the time, if we were to pass over in silence, the names of Cibber, Woffington, Pritchard and Clive.

Mrs. Cibber's first appearance on the stage was as a singer ; in which capacity, the sweetness of her voice, and the strength of her judgment, rendered her very soon conspicuous. Her first attempt as an actress was in the year 1736, in the character of Tara, in Mr. Hill's tragedy of that name, being the first night of its representation ; in which part she gave both surprise and delight to the audience, who were no less charmed with the beauties of her present performance, than with the prospect of future entertainment, from so valuable an acquisition to the stage ; a prospect which was to the end of her days perfectly maintained, and a meridian lustre shone forth equal to what was promised from the morning dawn. Her person was perfectly elegant, and when she was even declined beyond the bloom of youth, and even

wanted that *embonpoint*, which sometimes is assistant in con-
cealing the impression made by the hand of time, yet there was
so complete a symmetry and proportion in the different parts
that constituted this lady's form, that it was impossible to view
her figure and not think her young, or look in her face and not
think her handsome.   Her voice was beyond conception plaintive
and musical, yet far from deficient in powers for the expression
of resentment, and so much equal command of features did she
possess for the representation of pity or rage, of complacence or
disdain, that it would be difficult to say whether she affected the
hearts of the audience most, when playing the gentle, the delicate
Celia, or the haughty, the resenting Hermione; in the innocent
love-sick Juliet, or in the forsaken, the enraged Alicia.   In a
word she was excellent and inimitable in every cast of tragedy.
She made some attempts latterly in comedy, which were not, however, in any degree equal to her excellence in the opposite walk.
She departed this life the 30th of January, 1766, to the great
regret of every admirer of theatrical merit, having left no one
behind her that promises soon to supply her place with equal
abilities.

Mrs. Woffington may be considered entirely as an original in
her way; at the same time that she was an excellent actress in
genteel comedy, and even in tragedy, there was no woman that
ever yet had appeared upon the stage, who could represent with
such ease and elegance the character of a man.   Every one who
remembers her must recollect that she performed Sir Harry
Wildair, in the *Trip to the Jubilee*, far superior to any actor of
her time.   She was so happily made, and there was such symmetry and proportion in her frame, that she would have borne
the most critical examination of the nicest sculptor.   She had
besides dispossessed herself of that awkward stiffness and ef-
feminacy which so commonly attend the fair sex in breeches.   In
fine, she was the perfect contrast of the much celebrated Knayston,
who, in King Charles's time, so successfully appeared in all the
female characters, that it was a most nice point to decide between
the gentlemen and ladies, whether she was the finest woman or
the prettiest fellow.

We now approach a lady whose virtue was always irreproach-
able, and who has been as great an ornament to the stage as she
was an honour to her sex.   It were scarcely necessary after this
to repeat her name, or say, I mean Mrs. Pritchard.   If her figure
is not so happily suited to the juvenile, gay and volatile characters,
she has so melodious an elocution, so just an action, such expressive features, and with all that *je ne scai quoi*, which her

judgment so properly unites that we frequently forget Mrs. Pritchard is not eighteen, or that her waist is something more than half a yard round. In a word she is the only legal successor of Mrs. Oldfield, and in all her cast of parts is a most judicious and engaging actress.

Mrs. Clive whose maiden name was Raftor, was born in the year 1711, and displayed a very early inclination and genius for the stage. Her natural love of humour, and her pleasing manner of singing songs of spirit, induced some friends to recommend her to Colley Cibber. Her first appearance was in boy's clothes, in the character of a page in the tragedy of *Mithridates, King of Pontus*, in which she was introduced only to sing a song. Yet even in this she met with great applause. This was in the year 1728, at which time she was but seventeen years of age; and in the very same season we find that the audience paid so great attention to her merit in the part of Phillida, in Cibber's *Love in a Riddle*, which was damned, that they let her always peaceably go through her part. In the year 1730, she had an opportunity of displaying most amazing comic powers in the character of Nell, in the *Devil to Pay*. Her merit in this character occasioned her salary to be doubled, and not only established her own reputation with the audience, but fixed the piece itself on the constant list of acting farces; an honour which, perhaps, it would never have arrived at, had she not performed the capital character in it, nor may long maintain, when her support in it is lost. To expatiate on her merits as an actress, whilst she keeps within the extensive walk which is adapted to her excellence, would carry me far beyond my design, and indeed be superfluous to those who have ever seen her in these characters.

It is very remarkable that Mr. Quin and this last mentioned lady could never agree while they were united in the same company. There are several *bon mots* fathered upon him, which he is said to have spoken upon her account but they are of far too coarse and indelicate a character to find a place here. I am sorry to say that Quin's wit knew no bounds and that he was frequently severe and immodest even to the ladies. It is, indeed, averred, but upon what foundation I will not take upon me to say that the first disgust Quin took to this lady was upon his taking some liberties with her in her dressing room; she made a complaint to the manager, who rebuked him for his conduct.

CHAPTER X.

Mr. Garrick's theatrical pursuits. Mr. Rich's contemptible opinion of actors. The mild treatment the French players met with in 1748, and the severe treatment of the foreign dancers in 1755. Modern theatrical tumults and their causes, &c.

MR. GARRICK acted but one season at Goodman's Fields, notwithstanding the crowded and polite audiences he attracted thither from the west end of the town. Having very advantageous proposals made him from Dublin, he repaired to that city in the summer of the same year, where he found the like tribute to his merit, as he had received from his own countrymen. To the service of the latter, however, he esteemed himself more immediately bound, and therefore in the ensuing winter engaged himself with Mr. Fleetwood at Drury Lane, where he continued to perform till the year 1745; in the winter of which he again went over to Ireland, and continued there through the whole of that season, being a joint manager with Mr. Sheridan in the direction and profits of the Theatre Royal, in Smock Alley. From thence he returned to England, and was engaged for the season of 1746, with the late Mr. Rich at Covent Garden, where he played Ranger in Dr. Hoadley's *Suspicious Husband*, and Fribble in his own farce of *Miss in her Teens*. This however was his last performance as an hired actor; for in the close of that season, Mr. Fleetwood's patent for the management of Drury Lane being expired, and that gentleman having no inclination to pursue farther a design, by which from his want of acquaintance with the proper conduct of it, or some other reasons, he had already considerably impaired his fortune; Mr. Garrick, in conjunction with Mr. Lacey, purchased the property of that theatre, together with the renovation of the patent; and in the winter of 1747 opened with the best part of Mr. Fleetwood's former company, and the great additional strength of Mr. Barry, Mrs. Cibber, and Mrs. Pritchard from Covent Garden. These with Mr. Garrick and Mr. Quin, had all acted together the preceding winter at Covent Garden; but now Mr. Rich had no capital performer remaining but Mr. Quin, who never after quitted him, till he retired from the stage.

Mr. Garrick, upon the opening of Drury Lane theatre under his management, spoke an excellent prologue, which was written by

Mr. Samuel Johnson and which concluded with this address to the town :

"Then prompt no more the follies you decry,
As tyrants doom their tools of guilt to die ;
'Tis yours, this night, to bid the reign commence
Of rescued nature and reviving sense ;
To chace the charms of sound, the pomp of show,
For useful mirth and salutary woe ;
Bid scenic virtue form the rising age,
And truth diffuse her radiance from the stage."

Nothwithstanding so formidable a company were united at Drury lane, under Mr. Garrick's banner, Quin alone brought full houses for a whole season at Covent Garden, and Rich was pleased to say, that he was glad he had got rid of such turbulent servants, who were better paid than the admirals of his majesty's navy, without being of any advantage either to him or the state. If he had spoke his mind, he did not think Quin's presiding at the head of his company was of any great benefit to him ; for he attributed the good houses he had entirely to his *pantomimes* which he now *instructed* the town with and which he considered as a more rational entertainment than all Shakespeare's works together. This may perhaps be thought too severe by some of his friends, and it may be urged that though he gratified the vitiated of the town with *Harlequinades*, he was sensible that it was an invasion of Melpomene and Thalia's territories ; but the amazing expense he was at for scenes and decorations, his performing Harlequin still himself in some particular scenes ; his turning off three of his capital performers, and at length his dismissing Quin, will clearly prove that he looked upon pantomime as a superior kind of entertainment to either tragedy or comedy.

After the peace of Aix la Chapelle, which was concluded in 1748, a troop of French actors once more paid us a visit in our capital. They hired the little Theatre in the Haymarket upon their own account, and obtained a license for representing French plays. On the first night of their performance, there was a monstrous tumult, which seemed to threaten a total demolition, but the young men of quality, who did not choose to be interrupted in any diversion that had the royal license, broke the heads of such of the audience as opposed the performance and by the superiority of numbers, at length turned them ont. However the representation of French plays had but a very short run ; the manager was ruined, and the performers begged about the streets.

The French, or rather foreign, dancers did not meet with so mild a treatment at Drury Lane in 1755. It appeared by the list that was then printed, that there were not above two French-

men among them; but the cry was so great against them, that no
reason could be heard, and though this was the most magnificent
spectacle in the ballet way that ever was represented, they were
not suffered to proceed; and the audience not only pulled up the
benches in the pit, demolished the scenes and chandeliers, and
some of the sconces, but after having vented part of their rage at
the theatre, they repaired to Mr. Garrick's house in Southampton
Street, and broke every window in the front of it.   This attempt
to divert the town cost the managers, besides the expense of
scenery and decorations which they prepared for the representation, upwards of a thousand pounds, by the damage they
sustained from the depredations of the rioters.

From this time the theatres remained very peaceable till the
winter of the year 1762, and though it is rather antedating events
to mention it here, as I shall say but a few words upon it, the
reader will, it is hoped, pardon a small anachronism, to be no
farther disturbed hereafter with the tumults of the theatre.   The
subject of this disturbance was the non-admittance of half-price
to pantomimes.   But this was rather the pretext than the cause;
as the real source of this tumult might be traced to a misunderstanding between a certain Hibernian genius and Mr. Garrick,
after he had been the manager's guest and toad-eater for some
years; for having written a play, which was not approved of,
and therefore not acted, all his former adulation was turned
into scurrility and abuse; he attacked the manager in the public
newspapers, criticised his acting, censured his gesticulation, condemned his pronunciation and tortured his economy into parsimony
and meanness.

Not contented with this literary revenge, he waited for an opportunity to injure him in his property, and make him odious in
the eyes of the town.   An opportunity at length occurred, and
this individual, of no great consequence in life, had his vanity and
resentment so far gratified, as to give laws to both theatres with
respect to the prices of admittance.   These are so many cor-
roborating evidences of the inutility of the military power at the
theatres; and if we take a retrospective view of the history of
the stage from the time of the restoration of King Charles, and
the restoration of the drama, to the year 1721, when the military
aid was called in, we find there were few, if any, tumults at the
theatres before that period; and that such delinquents as were
refractory, and would disturb the amusement of the rest of the
audience, were more severely punished before, than since it took
place.

CHAPTER XI.

The quarrel between Rich and Quin impartially related. Quin leaves the
stage. His connexions and acquaintance. His generous behaviour
to Mr. Thomson. The effect of speaking the prologue to
Coriolanus.

WE now approach that period, when Mr. Quin's loss to the stage
was in many respects irreparable. At the end of the winter of
the year 1748, Quin, having taken umbrage at Rich's behaviour,
retired in a fit of spleen and resentment to Bath, notwithstanding
his being under engagements to that manager. Though Rich
ought to have known that Quin never put up with any insult and
though he too late repented of what he had done, yet he thought
by treating him with silent contempt, to make him submit to his
own terms. On the other hand, Quin, whose generous heart
began now to relent, having used his old acquaintance so cavalierly,
resolved to sacrifice his resentment to his friendship, and wrote
early the next season a laconic epistle to Rich in these words :

I am at Bath. QUIN.

Rich thought this by no means a sufficient apology for his behaviour, and returned an answer, in almost as laconic though not
quite so civil a manner,

Stay there and be d——d. RICH.

This reply cost the public one of the greatest ornaments of the
stage, for as he and Mr. Garrick did not agree very well together,
whilst they continued rival actors, he could not brook submitting
to his competitor in dramatic fame ; and as he now took a firm
resolution of never engaging again with *so insolent a blockhead*,
as he styled Rich for this answer, there was no theatrical door
open for him, without he had turned opera singer. He nevertheless came from Bath in the year 1749, to play the part of
Othello at Covent Garden theatre, for the benefit of the unhappy
sufferers by the fire in Cornhill, which happened on the 25th of
March, in the year 1748 ; and he afterwards continued many
successive years to come constantly to London, to perform the
character of Sir John Falstaff, for his old and trusty friend Ryan;
but in the year 1754, having lost two of his front teeth, he was
compelled to decline the task, and wrote a comic epistle to Ryan
upon the occasion.

My dear Friend,
        *There is no person on earth, whom I would sooner serve
than Ryan—but, by G——, I will whistle Falstaff for no man.*

Thus have we gone through the theatrical character of Mr. Quin,
who, having arrived at the summit of his profession, prudently
retired to a private retreat, where, if he did not add to the lustre
of his reputation as an actor, he avoided diminishing it as such,
and never sullied it as a man.   If he has not left behind him any
one who can fill his most important parts so perfectly as himself;
yet as long as Mr. Garrick chooses to indulge us with his performance, great justice will be done to Lear, Hamlet and Sir
John Brute; in Barry we may still find an Othello and a Jaffier;
in Mossop, a Zanga; and in Shuter, a Falstaff.

Whilst Mr. Quin continued upon the stage, he constantly kept
company with the greatest geniuses of the age; he was well known
to Pope and Swift, and the present Earl of C——d often invited
him to his table; but there was none for whom he entertained a
higher esteem than Mr. James Thomson, author of *The Seasons*,
and many dramatic pieces.   This genius had in the early part of
his life, by his writings, and the recommendations they gave him,
constantly enjoyed a very comfortable subsistence; he had
travelled as a companion with the honourable Mr. Charles Talbot
with whom he visited most of the courts of Europe, and returned
with his views greatly enlarged, not of exterior nature only, and
the works of art, but of human life and manners, and of the con-
stitution and policy of the several states, their connexions and
their religious institutions.   Upon his return to England, the
Chancellor, at Mr. Talbot's recommendation, made him his sec-
retary of briefs, a place of little attendance, suiting his retired
indolent way of life, and equal to all his wants.   This place fell,
when death not long after deprived him of his noble patron, and
he then found himself reduced to a state of precarious dependence;
in this situation, having created some few debts, and his creditors
finding that he had no longer any certain support, became inexorable and imagined by confinement to force that from his
friends which his modesty would not permit him to ask.

One of these occasions furnished Mr. Quin with an opportunity
of displaying the natural goodness of his heart, and the dis-
interestedness of his friendship.   Hearing that Thomson was
confined in a spunging-house, for a debt of about seventy pounds,
he repaired to the place, and having enquired for, was introduced
to the bard.   Thomson was a good deal disconcerted at seeing
Quin in such a place, as he had always taken great pains to con-
ceal his wants, and the more so as Quin told him he was come to

sup with him, being conscious that all the money he possessed would scarce procure a good one, and that there was no credit to be expected in those houses.   His anxiety upon this head was however removed, upon Quin's informing him, that as he supposed it would have been inconvenient to have had the supper dressed at the place they were in, he had ordered it from an adjacent tavern ; and as a prelude, half a dozen of claret was introduced.   Supper being over, and the bottle circulating pretty briskly, Quin said, "It is time now we should balance accounts :" this astonished Thomson, who imagined he had some demand upon him—but Quin perceiving it, continued, " Mr. Thomson, the pleasure I have had in perusing your works, I cannot estimate at less than a hundred pounds, and I insist upon now acquitting the debt :" on saying this, he put down a note of that value, and took his leave without waiting for a reply.

By this means was Thomson released from confinement, and Quin had the pleasure to see him a few years after again in affluence, having obtained the place of surveyor-general of the Leeward Islands.   After this he wrote several dramatic pieces, amongst others his tragedy of *Agamemnon* which was acted with applause in 1738 ; and the tragedy of *Edward and Eleanora* which he prepared for the stage the ensuing year, when he was refused a license for it.   Coriolanus was the last dramatic piece he wrote, and had not yet been acted, as the prologue testifies, at the time of his death in 1748.   This pleasing poet's principal merit not lying in the dramatic way, and this, though the last, being far from the best of his works, even of that kind, I cannot pay any very exalted compliments to the piece : yet in justice to the amicable character of its author, I must not avoid calling to mind in this place, the grateful tribute of sensibility paid to his memory at the first representation of it ; when, on a recapitulation of his loss in the prologue in a manner peculiarly affecting, and not without the visible tear trickling down his cheek,

> " I come not here your candour to implore,
> For scenes whose author is—alas ! no more.
> He wants no advocate his cause to plead ;
> You yourselves will be patrons of the dead ;"—

scarce an eye but began to moisten, and ere he had finished the prologue, a tributary tear was bestowed by almost every spectator, so general was the sense shewn of the value of a good and moral man.

CHAPTER XII.

The attention that was paid Mr. Quin by the late Prince of Wales. Is
appointed tutor for the English language to his royal highness's
children. They perform plays under his tuition. His extatic
exclamation upon a public occasion. His encounter with
Theophilus Cibber at the Bedford coffee-house. His
retreat to Bath, and manner of living there.

MR. QUIN had, during the course of his acting, from his judgment
in the English language, and the knowledge of the history of
Great Britain, corrected many mistakes which our immortal bard
Shakespeare had by oversight, or the volatileness of his genius,
suffered to creep into his works; he also changed many obsolete
phrases in his favourite poet, and restored the proper pronunciation of various words to the stage, from whence it had long
been banished.   These talents joined to his merits as an actor re-
commended him to the observation of his late royal highness the
Prince of Wales, father to his present Majesty, who appointed
him to instruct his children in the true pronunciation of their
mother tongue.   In order to accomplish this the more effectually,
it was necessary they should accustom themselves to the reading
of Milton, and some of our best dramatic poets; this naturally
created in them a desire to perform the parts they rehearsed;
and his late royal highness, who was a tender and indulgent
father, readily gratified their inclination.   Mr. Quin perfected
his royal pupils in their parts, and his present Majesty, with his
brothers and sisters, represented several plays under his tuition
at Leicester-house.

Nothing could surpass the joy he felt, when he was from time
to time informed of the virtuous and gracious disposition of his
royal pupil, contemplating with pleasure the felicity of the nation
under so good and just a prince; and upon being informed with
what elegance and noble propriety his Majesty delivered his
first gracious speech from the throne, he cried out in a kind of
ecstasy—" Ay—I taught the boy to speak !"—Nor did his
Majesty forget his old tutor, though so remote from court; for it
is positively averred, that soon after his accession to the throne,
he gave orders, without any application being made to him, that
a genteel pension should be paid Mr. Quin during his life.   It is
true, that Mr. Quin was not in absolute need of this royal bene-

faction; for, upon quitting the stage, he thought it was prudent to make some provision for the remainder of his days, and as he was never married, and had none but distant relatives, he resolved to sink half of his small fortune in order to procure an easy competence. The Duke of B——, who always professed a great regard for him, hearing of his design, sent for him, and. very generously told him, that he would grant him an annuity for his life upon very much better terms than any he could procure from persons who made a profession of granting annuities; and so in reality he did, for Mr. Quin obtained two hundred pounds a year for two thousand pounds. With this provision and about two thousand more he had in the funds, he retired to Bath, a place he had always in his eye for a retreat, as the manner of living, and the company that associated there, were so entirely consonant to his plan of life; he accordingly hired a house there, and had it fitted up in a decent, if not elegant, manner.

We may now suppose Mr. Quin at Bath; but before we fix him there for good, we must relate an adventure that happened at the Bedford coffee house about this time. The. Cibber, whose impertinence constantly kept pace with his vanity, having taken something amiss that Quin had said concerning his acting, came one night strutting into the coffee house, and having walked up to the fireplace, he said, "He was come to call that *capon-loined rascal* to an account for taking liberties with his character." Somebody told him, that he had been passed by Quin, who was sitting at the other end of the room in the window. "Ay, so I have sure enough" says he "but I see he is busy talking to Rich, and I won't disturb them now, I'll take another opportunity." "But," continued his informer, finding the backwardness of Cibber, and willing to have some sport, "he sets off for Bath to-morrow, and may not, perhaps, be in town again this twelve-month."—"Is that the case," said Cibber (somewhat nettled at finding his courage was suspected) "Then I e'en chastise him now."—Upon this he goes up to Quin and calls out aloud, "You— Mr. Quin, I think you call yourself, I insist upon satisfaction for the affront you gave me yesterday—demme"—"If you have a mind to be flogged," (replied Quin) "I'll do it for you with all my heart, d—mn me." "Draw Sir," resumed Cibber, "or I'll be through your guts this instant."—"This (said Quin) is an improper place to rehearse Lord Foppington in; but if you'll go under the Piazza, I may, perhaps, make you put up your sword faster than you drew it." Cibber now went out; Quin followed, when they immediately drew—Cibber parried, and retreated as

D

far as the garden rails, when Quin tired with trifling so long, made a lunge, in doing which he tumbled over a stone : Cibber taking the advantage of the accident, made a thrust at him, slightly wounded him in the forehead, and ran off full speed towards the church, as if for sanctuary.

Cibber put to flight, and Quin's wound dressed, the latter set out, according to his intention, the next day for Bath ; and now let us take a view of his manner of living in this city: to do this, it will be necessary to observe how people in general pass their time here. It is customary to begin the morning by bathing, which continues from six till about nine; the company then repair to the pump-house, some to drink the hot waters, but more for pastime, as they are here amused by a band of music, which fills up the intervals of wit and pleasantry. From hence the ladies withdraw to the female coffee house, and from thence to their lodgings to breakfast; the gentlemen at the same time withdraw to their coffee houses to read the papers, and converse upon the news of the day, or such topics as may occasionally occur ; and it must be acknowledged that this is done with a freedom and ease not to be met with in the coffee or chocolate houses of this city, for all restraint is there laid aside, and every one looks upon the present company as he would a set of old acquaintance whom he had known for many years. Public breakfasts are often given by persons of rank at the assembly houses, and sometimes private concerts. There are also in the morning lectures read upon various branches of arts and sciences for those who are inclined to improve their knowledge or refresh their memories. At noon the company appear upon the Parade and other walks, when they form parties for card playing or dancing for the evening. The more studious may now amuse themselves at the bookseller's shops, to which and the coffee houses, where they are allowed the use of pen and paper, they subscribe upon their arrival. We may now suppose it dinner-time, and if our friend partook of all the exercises of the morning, he was not behindhand in playing a pretty good knife and fork ; as Bath is furnished with elegant provisions of every kind, and excellent cooks. Dinner being finished, the company meet again at the pump-house, when, if fine weather, they adjourn to the walks and from thence repair to the assembly to drink tea. The evening concludes according to their respective engagements, either in visiting, at the play, or the ball. Thus Bath yields a continued rotation of diversions, and people of all ways of thinking, even from the libertine to the methodist, have it in their power to complete the day with employment agreeable to their taste and disposition.

Quin, who moved in the happy medium between both, could doubtless avail himself of the pastimes this agreeable place affords; if he did not often rise at six to bathe, or drink hot water in the pump-room, for the sake of being in fashion, he could enjoy the sprightliness of the conversation, and join in with the humourist or the satirist; he could comment upon the news of the day, with the politician or the schemist, at the coffee house; take a turn with Flirtilla upon the parade at noon; enjoy his friend and his mutton at three; crack a bottle and smoke his pipe till tea time; play a sober game at whist at the rooms; and retire contented to bed, without his losses or gains interrupting his repose.

CHAPTER XIII.

The calumnies invented of Mr. Quin during his residence at Bath. A
Refutation of them. The merit of the celebrated Beau Nash placed
in its true light.

SUCH then is the life which Mr. Quin passed for upwards of
sixteen years at Bath, without any interruption to his ease,
contentment, pleasantry and humour; though he was not without
his calumniators, his satirists, and even his murderers; for he
was many times put to death, even in the public papers long
before he really departed this life.

> " Envy does merit as its shade pursue,
> And as a shadow, proves the substance true."

The witlings of Bath constantly buzzing about him, to catch each
accent falling from his tongue, in order to pass it current for their
own, were not content with robbing him of his wit, but more than
once attacked his reputation; for not to mention the ridiculous
reports of his marriage at church, where they would insinuate he
had not been for many years, what but the highest pitch of
malice could have framed the report which was spread of his
design to supplant beau Nash, during his life, in the post of
Master of the Ceremonies? As this affair has made some noise,
and has already appeared in print, it will be necessary to consider
it with more attention than reports of a less serious nature.

A person of Nash's acquaintance in London, who pretended to
have great influence with Lord C——, informed him by letter,
that Quin was interceding to supplant him in his post of Master
of the Ceremonies; and to give this some colour, he transmitted
to him at the same time a letter, supposed to be written from
Quin at Bath to his lordship in town, which was under a flying
cover, to be transmitted to my lord by Nash's correspondent. It
is amazing that this officious friend to the old beau could so far
build upon his credulity and want of discernment, as to impose
upon him such a letter as he made Quin write to my lord, as the
grammar and spelling must at once have detected the imposition
to a person who would give himself a moment's time to reflect;
and yet Nash was so far imposed upon, as to print the letter
verbatim, and disperse it, in order to expose Quin's insincerity

and ignorance, without considering that they recoiled with double force upon himself.

We find the letter inserted in Nash's life, lately printed; and as the reader will certainly not be displeased to see it here, in order to clear Mr. Quin from the imputation of being its author, we shall transcribe it in the dress we there meet with it.

The letter from the intermediate correspondent to Mr. Nash, is as follows:

Dear Nash,   *London, Oct. 8, 1760.*

Two posts ago I received a letter from Quin, the old player, covering one to my lord, which he left open for my perusal, which after reading, he desired I might seal up and deliver. The request he makes is so extraordinary that it has induced me to send you the copy of his letter to my lord, which is as follows:

My dear Lord,   *Bath, Oct, 3, 1760.*

Old beaux Knash has made himselfe so disagreeable here to all the company that comes here to Bath, that the Corporation of this City have it now under their consideration to remove him from being Master of the Ceremoines, should he be continued, the inhabitants of this city will be ruined, as the best company declines to come to Bath on his account.

Give me leave to show to your lordship how he behaeved at the first ball he had here thiss season which was Tu'sday last. A younge lady was ask'd to dance a minuet.—She begg the gentleman would be pleased to exquise here, as she did not chuse to dance; upon this old Nash call'd out so as to be heard by all the company in the room—G— d—m yo Madam, what business have yo here, if you do not dance—upon which the lady was so affrighted she rose and danced,—the ress'et of the companey was so much offended, that not one lady more would dance a minueat that night. In the country dance no person of note danced except two boys Lords S— and T—, the rest of the companey that danced waire only the families of all the haberdashers, machinikes, and innkeepers in the three kingdoms, brushed up and colexted together. I have known upon such an occasion as this seventeen Dutchesses and Contisses to be at the opening of the ball at Bath, now not one. This man by his pride and extravigancis has outliv'd his reasion, it would be happy for thiss city that he was ded; and is now only fit to reed Shirlock upon death by which he may save his soul, and gaine more than all the proffits he can make, by his white hatt, suppose it was to be died red.

The favour I have now to request by what I now have wrote yo, is that your lordship will be so kind as to speke to Mr. Pitt for to

*recommend me to the Corporation of this City to succede this old
Sinner as Master of the Cerremonies and yo will much oblige.*

*My Lord your
Lord's Humble and
Obedient Servant.*

*N.B.   There was some other private matters and offers in
Quin's letter to my lord which do not relate to you.*

If it were necessary to prove, that it was impossible Mr. Quin
could ever write such a collection of unintelligible nonsense, it
would only require a comparison of the different parts of this
extraordinary epistle. In the first line the writer spells *Nash's*
name with a *K* and yet presently after he spells it right; the
author makes him write *dead* without the *a*, and yet he immediately spells *death* with the *a*; in one part he writes *ceremonies*
with the *i* before the *n*, and presently makes him put it in the
proper place; but to recompense for this *unintentional* correct-
ness he puts a couple of *r's*. It were indeed, needless to comment
upon so ridiculous a composition, which at the first view proves
itself an imposition and a forgery.

With respect to Quin's being desirous of obtaining the office of
Master of the Ceremonies at Bath, it will be only necessary to take
a short retrospect of the last fifteen years of his life: first his
retreat from the stage, by which he sacrificed between twelve and
fourteen hundred pounds a year, an income he could never expect
to gain in quality of Master of the Ceremonies; secondly, his
declining to appear in public for even his friend Ryan, on account
of his age and infirmities; and thirdly upon Nash's death, his not
taking the least step that indicated a desire of becoming his
successor; a design he might then, no doubt, have easily
accomplished, as it was at that time an employ that almost went
a begging. As I imagine the reader is by this time thoroughly
convinced that Mr. Quin was neither the author of the letter
attributed to him, or any way desirous of supplanting Nash as
Master of the Ceremonies, we shall dismiss the subject with a
short remark, which is, that Nash must at the time he took so
much pains to circulate this imposition, have been upon the verge
of dotage; and that doubtless, the suspicion he had of Quin's
being the real author, joined to the latter's resentment for
entertaining so mean an opinion of him, must have occasioned
that coldness which continued between them till the time of
Nash's death, as they never had any open rupture, or any private
misunderstanding, besides this, that ever transpired.

As I have been obliged through impartiality to censure Mr.

Nash's conduct in this affair, I will in turn acknowledge his merits, and must own that no man was ever better calculated than himself for the office he filled, so long as his memory and other abilities were unimpaired by age; for it is certain, that he greatly polished the manners of the age, and brought Bath to that regularity and perfection which we now see it, not without many struggles against prejudice and custom.   It is true, he soon prevailed upon the ladies to discontinue wearing aprons, by a piece of effrontery that would have been highly resented in any other person, but as King of Bath he reigned with absolute sway. He one night stripped off the Duchess of Q—nsb—y's apron, and threw it upon one of the back benches amongst the ladies maids, saying, "That aprons were only fit for Abigails to appear in." But the men were more refractory, and it was sometime before he could bring them to obedience; they would frequently appear at the ball in boots, and would generally come to the rooms with swords.   The first impropriety he rallied them out of by the representation of a puppet-show, where Punch appeared booted and spurred, in the character of a country squire, and upon his wedding night was going to bed with them on; when his lady remonstrated at his extravagance, he replied, "You may as well bid me pull off my legs—I ride in boots—I dance in boots—I do everything in boots—it is all the fashion at Bath and I never intend to quit them as long as I live."   Though this *burlesque* had its desired effect, he had not yet succeeded in his design upon swords, when an affair happened at Bath, which proved so powerful an auxiliary to him, that he beat them out of the field without any other weapons than common sense and reason.   The affair here mentioned was as follows: Two gamesters, whose names were Clarke and Taylor, fought a duel by torchlight in the grove.   Taylor was run through the body, but lived seven years after, at which time his wound breaking out afresh, it caused his death.   Clarke from that time pretended to be a Quaker, but the orthodox brethren never cordially received him among their number, and he died some years after in poverty and contrition. The rashness of a losing gamester is not now so much to be dreaded at Bath, and a man may escape with his life after the loss of his fortune.

CHAPTER XIV.

Some secret history, and original poetry; with animadversions, remarks,
comparisons, &c., &c., &c.

In the last chapter it was necessary to state some facts, and
examine them with impartiality, that a proper judgment might
be formed of the integrity of Mr. Quin, and the malignity of his
enemies. We are now going to relate a fact that will in some
degree corroborate what has just been supported; that is, in how
unimportant a light he considered the post of Master of the
Ceremonies at Bath, to which Nash alone could communicate
consequence, by his being so peculiarly formed to fill it, and give
it, at least an imaginary dignity.

It is well known at Bath, that when Nash was by the
inexorable tyrant compelled to relinquish his ideal crown, the
present Master of the Ceremonies, was not even thought of as
his successor. Mr. D—— being, however, at that time accidentally
at Bath, and having lately complimented a certain noble lord in
a poem, he, half in jest and half in earnest, said, "Suppose we
make D—— King of Bath; this proposal was seconded by two
or three ladies, who had been obliquely praised in the same piece,
and they imagined it would be no small feather in their cap if
they could say they had the Master of the Ceremonies for their
panegyrist. Accordingly, Mr. D—— was, by these ladies' interest,
without opposition elected.

Though Mr. D—— did everything in his power to render
himself agreeable, there still remained some objections to his
person and abilities; and upon a certain woman of fashion being
overlooked in the making up of a party, the clamour was so
strongly raised against him, that it was agitated whether or no he
should not be deposed; but as everything must be done with a
grace at Bath, a conference was held to determine in what
manner he should be *remerçie*. No one was supposed to understand punctilios of this sort better than Quin, and he was
accordingly consulted. "My lord," said he to the nobleman who
applied to him, "If you have a mind to put him out, do it at once,
and clap an extinguisher over him."

Quin's advice was taken, and Mr. D—— was for a time
supplanted by Monsieur —— who with all the abject servility
and *outree politesse* for which his countrymen are so celebrated
could not give so much satisfaction as his poetical predecessor.

Mr. D—— during his banishment, was assiduously employed in canvassing for favour and protection from his former patrons, the next season, and he exerted his talents to ridicule those who had been instrumental in dethroning him. Quin appeared to him, by the advice he gave as one of the most formidable and dangerous of his enemies; and he could not, therefore, let him escape the lash of his satirical pen. An Epigram which Mr. D—— wrote upon this occasion, and which was handed about at Arthur's, Lady N——'s rout, and of which a very few copies were obtained, though it never yet appeared in print, will, doubtless, be acceptable to the reader, as he may rely on its being genuine.

AN EPIGRAM CORRECTED.

When Quin of all grace and all dignity void,
Murdered Cato the Censor, and Brutus destroyed,
He strutted, he mouth'd; you no passion could trace
In his action, delivery, or plum-pudding face;
When he massacred Comus the gay god of mirth
He was suffered because we of actors had dearth.
But when Foote with strong judgment, and true genuine wit
Upon all his peculiar absurdities hit;
When Garrick arose, with those talents and fire,
Which nature and all the nine muses inspire,
Poor Guts was neglected, or laughed off the stage
So bursting with envy and tortured with rage;
He damn'd the whole town in a fury and fled,
Little Bayes an extinguisher clapp'd on his head.
Yet we never shall Falstaff behold so well done,
With such character, humour, such spirit, such fun,
So great that we knew not which most to admire,
Glutton, parasite, pander, pimp, letcher, or liar;
He felt as he spoke, nature's dictates are true
When he acted the part, his own picture he drew.

Though it cannot with justice be said that this production did any great honour to the muse of Mr. D——, yet it must be owned that Quin was not a little nettled at it; and Mr. D—— would have found a very dangerous opponent in his irritated antagonist, if he had not fallen upon a lucky expedient to soften his resentment.

It was well known that Mr. Quin had a particular veneration for John Dory, and Mr. D—— having at this time an acquaintance at Plymouth, he wrote to him in the most pressing terms *not to fail upon his return to bring up as many John Dories as he could possibly cram in the post chaise; to take particular care to have them of the best kind that could be got; and that he would make him any possible return in his power, as his future welfare entirely depended on it.* The sea officer who was Mr. D——'s correspondent, executed his commission so completely and arrived so critically at Bath with his cargo, at a time that there were no John Dories to be had at any price in that part of the country, that Quin upon receiving the present, was perfectly reconciled to Mr. D—— and entirely forgave him for his satirical attempt in rhyme.

Quin having once professed a friendship for a person, never withdrew it, unless he had the most cogent reasons for his conduct ; so that D—— was now extremely elated with the prospect of Quin's protection, and thereupon renewed with additional assiduity his application to the leading nobility of Bath, in order to be reinstated in his former office. Nor were his hopes groundless, for from the moment it was known that Quin had given him his suffrage, every one eagerly endeavoured to follow his example ; and the little Monarch of Bath once more regained his throne.

There are many characters in life whose peculiarities are ornamental to them ; but which in men of a different stamp are ridiculous and disgusting. Nash was by nature, formed for all that ostentatious frivolity, so requisite in a Master of the Ceremonies : he was in everything original ;—there was a whimsical refinement in his person, dress and behaviour ; it was habitual to him, and therefore sat so easy upon him, that no stranger who came to Bath, ever expressed any surprise at his uncommon manner and appearance. Mr. D—— probably thought that when he succeeded him in office, foppery and extravagance were its necessary appendages. No man in England had ever thought of wearing a white hat before Nash, and the reason he gave for this peculiarity (for he did nothing without some plausible plea, at least to himself) was, that it might not be changed. Mr. D—— has put on the white hat, and alleged the same reason, though he has actually lost two, and is now consulting three hatters upon the proper cock of the third. Nash always wore his stock buckle in front, because he said he had a wen in his neck, which would be very painful to him if too much pressed. Mr. D—— has no wen *yet* in his neck, and therefore at present wears his stock buckle like other people ; but he is in great hopes one is forming. Nash in the severest winter, never wore his waistcoat buttoned, but his shirt-bosom was constantly visible ; Mr. D—— intends to attempt the same juvenile appearance, as soon as the weather grows warm and he can with safety lay by his flannel waistcoat.

Such strict conformity in Mr. D—— to his predecessor's conduct, must convince every one that he never intends making any innovations upon the public or private government with which he is intrusted ; and therefore every admirer of the pastimes and amusements of Bath may rest assured that though Nash and Quin are no more, *decency,* *good manners,* and *proper regulations* will still continue to prevail, while Mr. D—— remains in peaceable possession of his throne.

CHAPTER XV.

The good intelligence that latterly subsisted between Mr. Garrick and
Mr. Quin. Visits him every summer at Hampton; the peculiar
facetiousness of the company in the excursion of 1765; poetry
written upon the occasion. His illness; his death.

FROM the time that Quin retired from the stage, a good harmony
subsisted, and a regular correspondence was carried on between
Mr. Garrick and him, and when he paid a visit to his friends in
this metropolis once a year, as he generally did in autumn, he as
constantly passed a week or two at Mr. Garrick's villa, at
Hampton. His last excursion thither in the summer of 1765,
was productive of the most agreeable sallies of wit and merriment: Mr. Garrick's travels furnished such new and entertaining
topics of discourse, and Mr. Quin's remarks such unexpected
strokes of fancy, as enlivened the conversation to a degree that is
almost incredible. Mr.——the poet, had also his share in the
entertainment that was afforded, and besides a plenteous discharge
of that inexhaustible fund of ready wit which so spontaneously
flows from him, his poetical vein was raised to such a pitch that
he could not suppress some extempore lines which involuntarily
escaped him. This put the whole company into a poetical mood,
and gave birth to the following little pieces that have at different
times made their way to the public :—

QUIN'S SOLILOQUY ON SEEING DUKE HUMPHREY AT ST. ALBANS.

A plague on Egypt's arts I say!
Embalm the dead! on senseless clay
   Rich wines and spices waste!
Like sturgeon, or like brawn, shall I
Bound in a precious pickle lie,
   Which I can never taste ?

Let me embalm this flesh of mine
With turtle fat, and Bourdeaux wine,
   And spoil th' Egyptian trade!
Than Humphrey's duke more happy I—
Embalm'd alive, old Quin shall die,
   A mummy ready made.

THE BRITISH EPICURE.

Imitated from Horace.

I hate French cooks, but love their wine,
On fricassee I scorn to dine,
    And bad's the best ragout :
Let me of claret have my fill,
Let me have turtle at my will,
    In one large mighty stew !

A napkin let my temples bind,
In night gown free and unconfin'd,
    And undisturbed by women !
All vows in one I ask of fate,
Behind the 'Change to eat my weight !
    And drink enough to swim in !

———

TO MR. QUIN

Upon his sending for his spectacles which he had left at Mr. Garrick's.

He that is robb'd, not *wanting* what is stolen,
Let him not *know't*, and he's not robbed at all.—OTHELLO.

———

From Shakespeare's law there's no appeal
To shew what *is*, what *not* to steal.
To keep the spectacles you left
As you must *want* them, would be *theft ;*
Your sight, alas, the worse for wear
Your *spectacles* you cannot spare ;
But when, my friend, you leave behind
Strong tokens of a vigorous mind ;
That coin, which never false or light,
That sterling *wit* you pay at sight ;
That *humour* trolling from your tongue,
So bold, emphatical and strong ;
That various whim, that social glee,
The quick enlivening repartee,
Jack Falstaff's rich variety !
Such, when you leave, to you *unknown*
Without a theft I make my own.
You can't be *robb'd* yourself must grant,
Of what you neither *miss* nor *want.*

STANZAS

Occasioned by the report of Mr. Garrick's quitting the stage,
and by seeing his epigram on Quin.

Long had the town her Garrick's absence mourned,
  And woo'd fair health with many an anxious prayer;
Till to his breast the blooming nymph return'd,
  Borne on the bright wings of Hesperian air.

But, ah! severe the cautious law she gave!
  What long reluctant Britain must deplore!
When her lov'd actor's favourite life to save,
  She bade him tread the wasting stage no more.

Grave look'd the god of laughter whilst she spoke;
  Of Lear's dim grave wild pity sought the gloom;
The mimic glass the muse of humour broke,
  And Shakespeare's genius languished o'er his tomb.

Phœbus was mov'd when Shakespeare's genius sigh'd,
  And nought he cried, the god of wit can give;
No grateful meed thy Garrick is denied:
  Then spare the actor, and the bard shall live.

But now, reader, you must prepare yourself to take a long farewell of your facetious acquaintance. During the stay he made at Hampton, he had an eruption on his hand, which the faculty were of opinion would turn to a mortification, and this intimation greatly damped his spirits, as the thought of losing a limb appeared to him more terrible than death itself; he therefore resolved, let what might be the consequence, not to suffer amputation. Whether this perspective so violently affected his spirits as to throw him into a hypochondria, or whether the natural bad habit of his body brought on a fever, this much is certain, that one of the malignant kind succeeded, and when he was out of all danger with respect to his hand, he was carried off by this fatal disorder.

During his illness he had taken such large quantities of bark, as to occasion an incessant drought, which nothing could assuage, and being willing to live as long as he could without pain, he discontinued taking any medicines for upwards of a week before his death, and during this period he was in very good spirits. The day before he died he drank a bottle of claret, and being sensible of his approaching end he said, "He could wish that the last tragic scene were over, though he was in hopes he should be able to go through it with becoming dignity." He was not mistaken, and departed this life on Tuesday, the 21st of January, 1766, about four o'clock in the morning, in the seventy-third year of his age.

The following is an authentic copy of his last Will and Testament :—

Mr. James Quin's last Will and Testament.

I JAMES QUIN, now residing in Bath, in the county of Somerset, Gent., being in good health and of sound and perfect mind and memory, do make and ordain this my last will and testament, in manner and form following :—

That is to say, after my funeral expenses and debts paid, I give and bequeath unto Mr. Thomas Nobbes, Oilman, in the Strand, London, five hundred pounds.

Item. I give and bequeath unto Mr. Charles Lowth, at the King's Head, in Paternoster Row, London, five hundred pounds.

Item. I give and bequeath unto Mr. Thomas James Quin, son of Dr. Henry Quin, Physician, in Dublin, one hundred pounds.

Item. I give and bequeath unto Mr. Anthony Pelham, Physician, now living in Southampton Street, Covent Garden, two hundred pounds.

Item. I give and bequeath, as by a very foolish promise, to Daniel Leekie, my gold repeating watch, chain, and seals.

Item. I give and bequeath to Mrs. Penelope Lepage, and to Mrs. Sarah Lepage, single or married, both nieces to the late Mrs. Forrester, fifty pounds each, or the whole hundred to the survivor.

Item. Unto William Grinsill, one of the Arts Masters of Bridewell Hospital, in London, five hundred pounds.

Item. I give and bequeath to Mr. Daniel Rich, of Sunning, near Reading, in the county of Berks., one hundred pounds.

Item. I give and bequeath unto Mr. Thomas Gainsborough, Limner, now living at Bath, fifty pounds.

Item. I give and bequeath unto the wife of Walter Nugent, a first Lieutenant in the Marines, fifty pounds.

Item. I give and bequeath unto Mr. Jeremiah Pierce, Surgeon, in Bath, my gold-headed crutch cane.

Item. I give and bequeath unto the Honourable Mr. John Needham, of Ivor, near Uxbridge, one hundred pounds.

Item. I give and bequeath unto Captain Robert Hughes, brother to the Commissioner at Portsmouth, fifty pounds.

Item. I give and bequeath unto Mrs. Mary Simpson, landlady of the Centre House, in Pierpont Street, in Bath, one hundred pounds ; to be paid by my executors into her own hands, independent of all her creditors whatsoever.

Item. I give and bequeath unto Mr. Edward Parker, Wine Merchant, in Bath, twenty guineas.

It is also my will that all the above legacies be paid and discharged within three months after my decease.

It is also my will to be privately interred.

All the rest and residue of my Estate, both real and personal, of what nature or kind soever, I give unto the above said Mr. Thomas Nobbes, and Mr. Charles Lowth, to enjoy to their use and behoof, to share alike, half and half. And I do hereby constitute and appoint the abovesaid Thomas Nobbes, Charles Lowth, and Edward Parker, to be the executors of and to this my last Will and Testament, hereby revoking and declaring void all former Wills by me made.

In Witness whereof, I the said James Quin have to this my last Will and Testament, contained in one sheet of paper, and written with my own hand, set my hand and seal this tenth day of July, in the year of our Lord, one thousand seven hundred and sixty-five.

JAMES QUIN. (L.S.)

Signed, sealed, published and declared, as and for the last Will and Testament of James Quin, in the presence of us who have hereunto subscribed our names in presence of each other, and in the presence, and at the request of the said James Quin,

HANBURY PETTINGAL,
JOSEPH PHILLOTT.

SUPPLEMENT.

CONTAINING

ORIGINAL FACTS AND ANECDOTES

RELATING TO THE LIFE OF QUIN.

ALSO

THE REMARKABLE TRIAL FOR THE MURDER OF MR. BOWEN.

COLLECTED AND ARRANGED FROM AUTHENTIC SOURCES.

WE shall now give in the form of an Appendix, some interesting matter respecting this celebrated actor, not included in the preceding work. In certain particulars this will be found to differ somewhat from the foregoing, as for instance, with respect to the fatal duel which involved Quin in such unpleasant consequences, but in the main it may be relied upon as more authentic, the information being drawn from the most reliable authorities; the account of the duel, in fact is taken from an ancient report of the trial at the Old Bailey, now seldom met with.

With regard to Quin's birth and the circumstances of his early life, there is some difference between the statements made by the few writers who have expressed themselves thereupon. The following facts related by accredited writers of various times may be read side by side and compared with the narrative already given.

This celebrated actor was born in King Street, Covent Garden, 24th Feb. 1693. His ancestors were of an ancient family in the kingdom of Ireland. His father, James Quin, was bred at Trinity College, Dublin, from whence he came to England, entered himself of Lincoln's Inn, and was called to the bar; but *his* father, Mark Quin, who had been Lord Mayor of Dublin in 1676, dying about that period, leaving him a plentiful estate, he quitted England in 1700, for his native country; taking with him his son, the object of our present attention.

The marriage of Mr. Quin's father was attended with circumstances which affected the future interest of his son so materially, as probably to influence his future destination in life. His mother was a reputed widow, who had been married to a person in the mercantile way, and who left her, to pursue some traffic or particular business in the West Indies. He had been absent from her near seven years, without her having received any letter from, or the least information about him. He was even given out to be dead, which report was universally credited; she went into mourning for him; and some time after Mr. Quin's father, who is said to have then possessed an estate of £1000 a year, paid his addresses to her and married her. The consequence of this marriage was Mr. Quin. His parents continued for some time in an undisturbed state of happiness, when the first husband returned, claimed his wife, and had her. Mr. Quin the elder retired with his son, to whom he is said to have left his property. Another, and more probable account, is that the estate was suffered to descend to the heir-at-law, and the illegitimacy of Mr. Quin being proved, he was dispossessed of it, and left to shift for himself.

Mr. Quin received his education at Dublin, under the care of Dr. Jones, until the death of his father in 1710, when the progress of it was interrupted, we may presume, by the litigations which arose about his estate. It is generally admitted that he was deficient in literature; and it has been said, that he laughed at those who read books by way of enquiry after knowledge, saying he read men—that the world was the best book. This account is believed to be founded in truth, and will prove the great strength of his natural understanding which enabled him to establish so considerable a reputation as a man of sense and genius.

Deprived thus of the property he expected and with no profession to support him, though he is said to have been intended for the law, Mr. Quin appears to have arrived at the age of 21 years. He had therefore nothing to rely upon but the exercise of his talents, and with these he soon supplied the deficiencies of fortune. The theatre at Dublin was then struggling for an establishment, and there he made his first essay. The part he performed was Abel in *The Committee*, in the year 1714; and represented a few other characters, as Cleon in *Timon of Athens*, Prince of Tanais in *Tamerlane*, and others, but all of equal insignificance. After performing one season in Dublin, he was advised by Chetwood not to smother his rising genius in a kingdom where there was no great encouragement for merit.

This advice he adopted and came to London, where he was immediately received into the company at Drury Lane. It may be proper here to mention, that he repaid the friendship of Chetwood by a recommendation which enabled that gentleman to follow him to the metropolis.

At that period it was usual for young actors to perform inferior characters, and to rise in the theatre as they displayed skill and improvement. In conformity to this practice, the parts which Mr. Quin had allotted to him were not calculated to procure much celebrity for him. He performed the Lieutenant of the Tower in Rowe's *Jane Grey ;* the Steward in Gay's *What d' ye Call It ;* and Vulture in *The Country Lasses :* all acted in 1715.

In December, 1716, he performed a part of more consequence, that of Antenor, in Mrs. Centlivre's *Cruel Gift ;* but in the beginning of the next year, we find him degraded to speak about a dozen lines in the character of the Second Player, in *Three Hours after Marriage.*

Accident, however, had just before procured him an opportunity of displaying his talents, which he did not neglect. An order had been sent by the Lord Chamberlain to revive the play of *Tamerlane,* for the 4th of November, 1716. It had accordingly been got up with great magnificence. On the third night, Mr. Mills, who performed Bajazet, was suddenly taken ill, and application was made to Mr. Quin to read the part ; a task which he executed so much to the satisfaction of the audience, that he received a considerable share of applause. The next night he made himself perfect, and performed it with redoubled proofs of approbation. On this occasion he was complimented by several persons of distinction and dramatic taste upon his early rising genius.

It does not appear that he derived any other advantage at the time from his success. Impatient, therefore, of his situation, and dissatisfied with his employers, he determined upon trying his fortune at Mr. Rich's Theatre, at Lincoln's Inn Fields, then under the management of Messrs. Keene, and Christopher Bullock ; and accordingly in 1717, quitted Drury Lane, after remaining there two seasons. Chetwood insinuates that envy influenced some of the managers of Drury Lane to depress so rising an actor. Be that as it may, he continued at the theatre he had chosen seventeen years, and during that period supported without discredit, the same characters which were then admirably performed at the rival theatre.

Soon after he quitted Drury Lane an unfortunate transaction

took place, which threatened to interrupt, if not entirely to stop
his theatrical pursuits; this was an unlucky rencounter between
him and Mr. Bowen, which ended fatally to the latter.

The account of this duel in which Quin mortally wounded his
adversary, and his indictment for the same, as narrated by the
writer of the treatise forming the first part of this work, is no
doubt in many respects somewhat inaccurate; we here give the
interesting and authentic report of the trial, with the evidence
then taken for and against the prisoner, published in the year
1721, in *A Compleat Collection of Remarkable Tryals of the most
Notorious Malefactors at the Sessions House in the Old Bailey,
from the year 1706, to the last Sessions 1720.*

The Trial, &c., of James Quinn, Gent.

He was indicted for the Murther of *William Bowen*, Gent., on
the 17th of April, 1718, by giving him one mortal Wound with a
Sword on the right side of his Belly, of the breadth of one Inch
and the depth of four Inches, of which Wound he languished till
the 20th, and then Died.   He was also indicted a second time
upon the Coroner's Inquest for Manslaughter.   The Evidence was
as followeth :—

Robert Martin deposd: That he being at the *Fleece Tavern*, in
Cornhill, the 17th of *April*, about 4 or 5 o'clock in the *Afternoon*, Mr. *Bowen* being there, and espying him, called to him and
desired him to drink a Glass of Wine with him, which he did,
and that then Mr. *Quinn*, was with Mr. *Bowen ;* that as they
drank, Mr. *Bowen* and Mr. *Quinn* put pretty smartly upon one
another with cutting jests, and fell to talk of their Performances
in Acting, whereupon Mr. *Quinn* told Mr. *Bowen, he had no
occasion to value himself so much on that score, since Mr. Johnson, who had but seldom acted it, did act the part of Jacomo
in the Libertine as well as he who had Acted it often.*   That from
this Discourse they fell into Discourse about their Honesty, and
Mr. *Bowen* giving himself the Character of *as honest a man as
any was in the World.*   To which Mr. *Quinn* replied by asking
Mr. *Bowen* if he should tell the Story of the Court, Mr. *Bowen*
said no, it was no matter; but at last said he might tell it if he
would, which Mr. *Quinn* did, and Mr. *Bowen* still persisting to
abide by the assertion of his Honesty, they proceeded so far as to
lay Wagers about it, and Money was laid down.   Mr. *Quinn*
charged Mr. *Bowen* with sometimes drinking Healths to the
Duke of Ormond and at other times refusing it.   Asking Mr.
Martin, to whom the Decision of the Wager was left; how

could he be as honest a man as any was in the World who acted upon two different Principles? That thereupon *Mr. Martin* told *Mr. Bowen*, that if he insisted upon it, as to his being as Honest a Man as any was in the World, he must needs give it against him. That this Discourse was all the while carry'd on with a jocular air, but upon this *Mr. Bowen* rose up, flung down some Money for the Reckoning, saying he could not bear it, but must be gone; that he did go away, but he did not perceive in him any Signs of a Resentment that should procure so fatal a Consequence; that after *Mr. Bowen* had been gone about a quarter of an hour, there came a Porter to the Fleece Tavern, to enquire for him, and asked if one *Mr. Quinn* was not in the Company; that *Mr. Quinn* went out to the Porter, and the Porter having whispered him in the Ear, he went away with him, and having been gone about a quarter of an Hour, *Mr. Quinn* came back and asked if he knew where *Mr. Bowen* lodged, desiring that they would go to the *Pope's Head Tavern*, and take care of him, for there had been a Dispute between them, and he was afraid he had wounded him mortally. That then *Mr. Quinn* went away, and he and *Mr. Day* who were then in Company, went immediately to the *Pope's Head Tavern*, and enquired for *Mr. Quinn* and *Mr. Bowen*, but the Porter of the Tavern said they did not know them, nor would own that *Mr. Bowen* was there; that sitting down to drink in an open Room next the passage, they saw a Chair brought in, and asking whether there was not a Gentlemen wounded there; they were answered, no, there was no Gentleman there wounded, but that Chair was for a Gentleman that was something disordered. That then a Gentleman came down stairs and went into the Chair, but the sight being intercepted by the Bar, they could not see him go in, but heard him say to the Man of the House, *I am wounded in your House, but it is done fairly, the Gentleman has done it fairly.*

Mr. Day deposed: That he having been with some Gentlemen at the *Fleece Tavern* was going Home, and in the Tavern Yard a Gentleman hipp'd to him, which was *Mr. Bowen*, who was sitting in a Room by himself; he desired him to drink a Glass of Wine with him, but he refus'd, not having Dined; but he going home, it being about 4 o'clock, the Family had Dined, whereupon he returned to the *Fleece*, and there found *Mr. Bowen*, *Mr. Quinn*, and *Mr. Martin* together. That *Mr. Bowen* and *Mr. Quinn* were talking together in a jocular manner about their performances in acting; and *Mr. Bowen* reflected on *Mr. Quinn*, that he had acted *Tamerlane* in a loose sort of a manner; that *Mr. Quinn* replied that *Mr. Bowen* had no great occasion to value himself for his Performance in that *Mr. Johnson* who had acted it but seldom, acted the part of *Jacomo* in *The Libertine* as well as he, who had acted it often. That from this discourse, by what transition he knew not, they fell into discourse about Honesty, and *Mr. Bowen* giving himself the Character of as honest a Man as any was in the World *Mr. Quinn* told a story : that having been out one Night pretty late and going home, he heard in a Court a hot Contention between a Gentleman and a Woman, which Gentleman he found to be *Mr. Bowen*, who in very high terms was demanding the return of half a Crown of her, which she was unwilling to part with ; but he swearing he would have it, she offered to give him back a Shilling of the Half Crown but he swore he would have it all ; then she offered him Eighteen-pence, but he insisting upon the whole, she told him it was very Ungentlemanlike to insist upon the whole, but he still insisting she offered Two Shillings, but he swearing he would have it all, he had it all back of her. The story being told, *Mr. Bowen* insisted still on his Honesty and that Nothwithstanding, he was as Honest a Man as any was in the World, and offered to lay a Wager on it, which *Mr. Quinn* would have evaded ; but *Mr. Bowen* urging it, *Mr. Quinn* said if you will lay I will lay you ; and the money was laid down on both sides, and *Mr. Martin* was to decide the Controversy. That *Mr. Quinn* then related some Passages of *Mr. Bowen's* Drinking the Healths of Persons obnoxious to the Government, and such like Matters and that *Mr. Martin* said, if I must give my Opinion as to your being as Honest a Man as any in the World, or in *England*, I must give it against you. That soon after *Mr. Bowen* in a hasty sort of a manner rose up and threw down some money, saying he would not stay in the Company any longer, and so went away. But he did not perceive any such high Resentments and Anger in him as to apprehend any such fatal Consequence ; the mutual Freedoms that were taken on both sides seeming to rise no higher than to cause the common Ruffles of Human Nature and not to be such as he would call *Mr. Quinn* to account for. That then *Mr. Bowen* having been gone a quarter of an Hour or less, a Porter came and enquired for *Mr. Quinn*, and he went away with the Porter, but they knew not that it was *Mr. Bowen* had sent for him, and in about a quarter of an Hour's time *Mr. Quinn* came back and said *Mr. Bowen* had sent for him to the *Pope's Head Tavern*, had taken Occasion to quarrel with him, had obliged him. to fight him, he had done so, and believed he had hurt him, and desired us to go see if it were mortal, and to take care of him. That immediately they went to the *Pope's Head Tavern*, as has been before related, but the People of the House denied *Mr. Bowen's* being there; but saw a Chair brought in, heard his voice when he was got into the Chair, saying to the Landlord, *I am wounded in your House, but the Gentleman has done it fairly. If I die I forgive him, but if I live I will be revenged of him.*

Tho. Antrum, the Porter, deposed: That as he was standing by *Tom's Coffee House,* in *Cornhill, Mr. Bowen* called to him and bid him go to the *Fleece Tavern* and ask for *Mr.*——, and seeming to have forgot the Name, swore as tho' in a fret, and went a little from him, then calling him again, bid him go and ask for *Mr. Martin,* and if *Mr. Quinn* was in the Company to tell him a Gentleman wanted to speak with him; that he did so, and *Mr. Quinn* came immediately out to *Mr. Bowen,* who had then walked about half-a-score Doors lower, and *Mr. Quinn* coming up to him they went both together into the *Swan Tavern,* but *Mr. Bowen* gave him nothing for his pains.

Henry Trevesa, Drawer at the *Swan Tavern,* deposed: That about six or seven o'clock at Night, the 17th of April, *Mr. Bowen* and *Mr. Quinn* came in together and asked for a Room, he shewed them a Room up one pair of Stairs, *Mr. Bowen* going up first, but that room having been new painted, *Mr. Bowen* objected to it, as smelling of Paint, he then showed them into the Great Room, which because there were some Gentlemen drinking at one end of it, *Mr. Bowen* said would not do, he turned about shaking his head, and seeming angry with him, went down Stairs and so away.

Mr. Griffin Bowen deposed: That about 11 o'clock at Night, the 17th of April, a Person came to him desiring him to go to his Father, for that he was wounded; upon which he went and found his Father in Bed. That he asked him several times how it came, and who had done it, but he would not tell him, but at last with much Urgency he said it was *Mr. Quinn.* To which he replied, *Is it that Man? The worst of all mankind! How came you into his Company? If you get over it, it will be a Reflection upon your Family.* That at that time they were not apprehensive that the Wound was Mortal; but on the Sunday, about Twelve or One o'clock, some Symptoms of Death appearing, as his Nails turning black, the Doctor being present told his Father he would have him think of another World, in that he was not a yard from Death. Whereupon he again urged him, as he was a dying Man, to tell him how the Accident came. To which he replied, that he met *Mr. Quinn* at the *Fleece Tavern,* in *Cornhill,* who was always abusive to him, and he having given him provoking Language there, he went away, and sent for him out to desire him not to give himself that freedom of Speech against him. That *Quinn* said he should go to the Tavern, and that they went to the *Swan*, and afterwards to the *Pope's Head*, where with a Volley of Oaths he gave him abusive Language, barricaded the Door with two Chairs, and he having given him such foul Language he could not bear, their Swords were drawn, and he catching *Mr. Quinn* by the Sword-arm he wrested himself from him and gave him that Wound.

Mary Sewel deposed : That she being present half-an-hour or an Hour before *Mr. Bowen's* Death, heard him being asked how it came, say, very unfairly, I was barbarously murthered.

Mr. Essex Weller deposed : That there had been for near two years standing, a misunderstanding between *Mr. Quinn* and *Mr. Bowen*, which he apprehended was occasioned as follows : that *Mr. Quinn* at his first coming into the Play-house, behaved himself with much civility and good manners, but soon after broke out into quite the reverse of it ; that *Mr. Bowen* taking upon him to advise him to another manner of behaviour, it was the occasion of a Difference between them, and since that time *Mr. Quin* had shewn an Animosity against *Mr. Bowen*, saying he was a vile Fellow, and was not fit to live ; used to call him Turn-coat, and would sometimes ask him if he did not drink the *Duke of Ormond's* Health in his Heart, and sometimes saying he ought to be used like a Dog, and deserved to be stuck. That this had continued for two Winters, till *Mr. Quinn* left the Company, and went to *Lincoln's Inn Fields* Play-house. It was further deposed, that as *Mr. Quinn* was sitting by the Fire behind the Scenes, and *Mr. Bowen* passed through, *Mr. Quinn* seeing him said, here comes that rascally, Whiggish, Tory Fellow, *Bowen*, who deserves to be stuck, but *Mr. Bowen* went on, not seeming to take any notice of it.

Jonas Mounsey, the Surgeon deposed : That on *Thursday* the 17th of *April*, he was sent for to the *Horn Tavern* in *Fleet Street* to dress *Mr. Bowen*, that he found a small wound under his arm and another in his Belly about four inches below the Navel, which he dressed, and being sent for to another Patient left him, not then apprehending it would be mortal ; but afterwards on the *Monday*, *Mr. Bowen* being dead, he opened him and found the Wound had gone several Inches into the Cavity of his Belly, slanting a little towards the left, and had touched a Gut, and was persuaded that Wound was the Cause of his Death.

Mr. Quinn in his defence pleaded : That he having accidentally met *Mr. Bowen* at the *Fleece Tavern* in *Cornhill*, they drank together in the Company, and had the Conversation that has been

before related; that thereupon *Mr. Bowen* went away, leaving
him in the Company of *Mr. Martin* and *Mr. Day*; that in about
a quarter of an Hour after a Porter came and asked for him
telling him a Gentleman wanted to speak with him; whereupon
he took up his Hat and Gloves, his Sword being then by his side,
and went away with the Porter, and in *Cornhill* about six doors
below the *Fleece* he found *Mr. Bowen*, who said he wanted to
drink a pint of wine with him: upon which he replied that if
Mr. Bowen had half an Hour to spare, he thought it were better
to spend it in the Company of those Gentlemen they had before
been in, adding likewise that he coming away with the Porter
had not paid his reckoning: but *Mr. Bowen* refused so to do,
saying he would go to the *Swan*; and *Mr. Bowen* asking for a
Room followed the Drawer up one pair of Stairs, and himself
followed *Mr. Bowen*, but the Room having been new painted, he
said it would not do. That then the Drawer shewed them the
Great Room, but there being some gentlemen in it, *Mr. Bowen*
said it would not do; the Drawer offered to draw a Curtain to
part the Companies, but *Mr. Bowen* saying it would not do, went
down Stairs, he following him. Then *Mr. Bowen* said he would
go to the *Pope's Head*, where being shewn a Room, and calling
for a Pint of Wine, they sat down, and he desired *Mr. Bowen* to
tell him what he had to say to him, desiring it might be short in
that he had left his Company without paying the Reckoning.
That then having drank each a Glass of Wine, he perceived a
Distortion in *Mr. Bowen's* Countenance, and he rose and barricaded the door with two chairs, told him that he had injured him
past verbal reparation, and nothing but fighting him should make
him amends. That thereupon he argued with him, endeavouring
to dissuade him, but *Mr. Bowen* bid him not trifle with him.
That he then desired *Mr. Bowen* again to defer his Resentment
and sleep upon it, and if he could not come into Temper by the
next day, he would meet him and ask his Pardon in the same
Company that he had injured him in; but *Mr. Bowen* bid him
again not trifle with him, for that he had injured him in his
Reputation, which he was resolved never to survive, and would
now do himself justice, and drawing his Sword in a violent
passion, swore if he did not draw he would run him through,
upon which he was obliged to draw in his own defence, and what
was the Consequence has been before related. That he having
given *Mr. Bowen* the wound, he took him by the hand, kissed
him, bid him take his Hat and Wig and go back to the *Fleece*,
and send *Mr. Martin* to him to take care of him, afterwards to
make his Escape, and if he died desired him to be a Father to

his Children. The Prisoner then called several Evidences who deposed as follows : Besides the Porter who deposed as before, that *Mr. Bowen* sent him to the *Fleece Tavern*, for *Mr. Quinn*, and the Drawer at the *Pope's Head Tavern*, deposed : That *Mr. Bowen* came and asked for a Room ; that he shewed him one ; that having carried in a Pint of Wine, filled a glass or two, set it down, and went away, and knew nothing of any encounter, or heard any noise, till about a quarter of an hour after *Mr. Bowen* rang the Bell ; he went up, *Mr. Quinn* was gone ; *Mr. Bowen* bid him go to the *Fleece Tavern* and call *Mr. Martin;* he went but *Mr. Martin* was gone ; he told *Mr. Bowen*, and he bid him call a Surgeon, but recalling him again, bid him fetch a Chair—leaning his head on the table, he called a Chair and went away in it, and at his going in said that what *Mr. Quinn* had done, he had done very honourably and justly, and that he heartily forgave *Mr. Quinn*, live or die.

Edward Meakins, the Master of the *Pope's Head Tavern*, deposed : That he being engaged with the Parish Officers then in his House, knew nothing of the matter till *Mr. Bowen* had gotten a Chair in order to go away ; that being in the Chair, *Mr. Bowen* desired to speak with him, telling him he was wounded in his House ; that then he desired him to send for a Surgeon, he replied he had, but he could not be found ; that *Mr. Bowen* added, *I sent for you to tell you, if I die, he has done me Justice, he gave me Fair-play; I freely forgive him.*

John Wright, Drawer, of the *Horn Tavern*, deposed : That *Mr. Bowen* came back about 7 o'clock in the Evening, to their House in a Chair ; that he went with him to *Steward's Coffee House*, and afterwards to the *Horn Tavern;* that he said he was wounded and desired him to fetch a Surgeon, which he did, who dressed him, and being called to another Patient, went away ; that then he asked *Mr. Bowen* who had wounded him ? He replied *Mr. Quin*, but said several times he had done it fairly, and he freely forgave him.

Prudence Inwell depos'd : That *Mr. Bowen* came to *Steward's Coffee House* in *Fleet Street*, supported by the Drawer of the *Horn Tavern*, he seemed very ill, and out of Order, and the Drawer said he was wounded : She asked him who had done it, he said he would not tell her, but he who did it had done it very fairly, and he freely forgave him. The Prisoner put a question to her, how *Mr. Bowen* had used to behave himself at her House; she answered, he was used to be often out of Humour and had oftentimes been very disturbing to the Company.

William Gadson depos'd : That he was at the *Coffee House* when *Mr. Bowen* came in, and that he said he was wounded, but the Gentleman that had done it, had done it fairly, and he freely forgave him.

Michael Owen, depos'd, that he seeing *Mr. Bowen* come into *Steward's Coffee House* in Disorder, did think he had been drunk and therefore said, *here comes Bowen in his old pickle*; but afterwards understood he was wounded, heard him say it was done fairly, and he freely forgave the Gentleman.

Mr. Cheret depos'd : That the next morning, he being in Company with *Mr. Wilks*, he told him that *Mr. Bowen* was killed, and that *Mr. Quinn* had killed him, and that *Mr. Bowen* had sent for him, but he did not much care for going, as *Mr. Quinn* had quitted their House, if he were brought in as Evidence to any matter, the World might imagine he shewed something of Spleen, but however *Mr. Bowen* in those Circumstances having sent for him he would go, and desired him to go with him ; that they did go, and *Mr. Bowen* desired of *Mr. Wilks*, that as there was a Play to be acted for his Benefit, if he Died his Wife and Children might have the benefit. That *Mr. Bowen* said *Mr. Quinn* had given him very ill Language that he could not bear ; that he had obliged him to draw his Sword, and then he received that wound; that when *Mrs. Bowen* talked of prosecuting *Mr. Quinn*, he desired she would not. *Mr. Cheret* also added, that *Mr. Bowen* and *Mr. Quinn* had often had Disputes, and always used to be jangling.

Then the Prisoner said : Whereas one *Mr. Weller* has given me a very ill Character, I shall produce to the Court one Reason for that Character, calling one *Mr. Reason*, who deposed, he had heard one *Mr. Weller* say, that if he could, he would be an Instrument of hanging *Mr. Quinn*, for he had quarrell'd with me and all the House. The Prisoner then added, that though he was unwilling to bring the Character of *Mr. Bowen's* past Life upon the Stage, yet it being necessary in his own Defence, he desired Leave of the Court to call *Mr. Francis Lee*, who deposed: That *Mr. Bowen* was a very quarrelsome man, and had several times attempted his Life, and once particularly as he was sitting at his Father's Door, *Mr Bowen* passed by him and asked him how he did, to which he civilly answered ; that *Mr. Bowen* passed on, went into a Coffee House, and coming back in about half-an-hour, while he was still sitting there, without any Provocation called him ill Names, drew his Sword, cut him over the Head, and he rising and retreating backward into the House he happened to fall, whereupon he made two Passes at him with his Sword, but happened to miss him, he putting it by with his hand,

and somebody coming by, and taking hold of him, he was
shortening his Sword to have stabb'd him as he lay on the ground,
but was prevented by Persons running to his Assistance. That
thereupon he advised with *Sir Peter King* in order to prosecute
him, and did, but by the Mediation of some Great Men on *Mr.
Bowen's* Account, did make it up with him. That he afterwards
did attack him in *Salisbury Court*, when he had no Sword, but
People coming to his assistance prevented him, upon which he
arrested him. That he afterwards broke into his chamber while
he and his Wife were in bed demanding satisfaction of him. He
added that *Mr. Bowen* met him about three days before he
received this wound by *Mr. Quinn*, and would needs drink a
Pint with him at the *Ship Tavern*, near *Temple Bar*, and there
told him, *Mr. Lee, you and I have had Difference but I desire you
to put it up, and as I am an older Man than you, shall probably
die before you, and I desire you to come to my Burial*, which at
last he promised him to do, but had then no Apprehension it
would be so soon.

Thomas Allpress confirmed the first Assault of *Mr. Bowen*
upon *Mr. Lee*, and that he seeing him push at him as he lay upon
the ground caught hold of him, and pulling him back prevented
him from stabbing him.

William Brown deposed : *Mr. Bowen* was always very fractious,
and that he coming into the *Sugar Loaf* Ale House, in *Fleet
Street*, saw *Mr. Bowen* with his Sword drawn, swearing and
making a great Disturbance ; that the Man of the House desired
him to go out, telling him he knew he would let him have no
Drink, having several times forbad him his House, he having
made a Difference between him and his Wife ; that he thereupon
persuaded him to go away and not be further troublesome ; he
was in great Passion with him, swearing at him, and saying, *you
prevented me in my Business and I will do yours for you.* That
he afterwards meeting *Mr. Bowen*, told him of it, to which *Mr.
Bowen* replied, *It is my Temper, I meant no hurt, you're a very
honest fellow.*

The Prisoner then call'd several Persons to his Reputation :

Mr. Theophilus Keen depos'd : That he had known *Mr. Quinn*
very well, always found him rather inclinable to make up than
promote Quarrels, and rather take those things others called
Affronts, than quarrelsomely resent them. This was confirmed
by *Mr. Bullock, Mr. King, Mr. Hawks, Mr. Moreton, Mr. Brown,
&c.* The Prisoner then added, I have done nothing but what I
was compelled to do, had I not opposed *Mr. Bowen's* Violence, I
must have been guilty of Self-Murther. The Jury upon con-

sidering the whole matter, found him Guilty of Manslaughter only. The affair seems to have been regarded very lightly, for *Quinn* soon after returned to his employment on the Stage, and in the course of time his well-known generosity effaced all recollection of it, or at any rate induced men to impute to him very little blame for his share in it.

The friendship between Mr. Quin and Mr. Ryan is well known, and it is something remarkable, that they were each at the same time embarrassed by a similar accident. We have already mentioned that Bowen received the wound which occasioned his death, on the 17th of April. On the 20th of June, Mr. Ryan was at the Sun Eating-house, Long Acre, at supper, when a Mr. Kelly, who had before terrified several companies, by drawing his sword on persons whom he did not know, came into the room in a fit of drunkenness, abused Mr. Ryan, drew his sword on him, with which he made three passes before Ryan could get his own sword, which lay in the window. With this he defended himself, and ran Mr. Kelly in the left side, who fell down, and immediately expired. It does not appear that Mr. Ryan was obliged to take his trial for this homicide.

The Theatre in which Mr. Quin was established, had not the patronage of the public in any degree equal to its rival at Drury Lane, nor had it the good fortune to acquire those advantages which fashion liberally confers on its favourites, until several years after. The performances, however, though not equal to those at Drury Lane, were far from deserving censure. In the season of 1718-19, Mr. Quin performed in Buckingham's *Scipio Africanus*, and in 1719-20, *Sir. Walter Raleigh*, in Dr. Sewell's play of that name; and in the same year had, as it appears two benefits, *The Provoked Wife*, 31st of January, before any other performer, and again, *The Squire of Alsatia*, on the 17th of April. The succeeding season he performed in Buckingham's *Henry the Fourth of France*, in *Richard II.*, as altered by Theobald, and in the *Imperial Captives*, of Mottley. The season of 1720-21, was very favourable to his reputation as an actor. On the 22nd of October, *The Merry Wives of Windsor*, was revived, in which he first played Falstaff, with great increase of fame. This play, which was well supported by Ryan, in Ford; Spiller, in Doctor Caius; Boheme, in Justice Shallow; and Griffin, in Sir Hugh Evans, was acted nineteen times during the season, a proof that it had made a very favourable impression on the public. In the season of 1721-22, he performed in Mitchell's, or rather Hill's *Fatal Extravagance ;* Sturmy's *Love and Duty ;* Phillip's *Hibernia Freed.* The season of 1722-23 produced

Fenton's *Mariamne*, the most successful play that theatre had known, in which Mr. Quin performed Sohemus. In the next year, 1723-24, he acted in Jeffrey's *Edwin*, and in Philips's *Belisarius*. The season of 1724-25 produced no new play in which Mr. Quin had any part; but on the revival of *Every Man in His Humour*, he represented old Knowell; and it is not unworthy of observation, that Kitely, afterwards so admirably performed by Mr. Garrick, was assigned to Mr. Hippesley, the Shuter, or Edwin of his day. In 1725-26, he performed in Southern's *Money's the Mistress ;* and in 1726-27, in Welsted's *Dissembled Wanton*, and Frowde's *Fall of Saguntum*.

For a year or more before this period, Lincoln's Inn Fields Theatre had, by the assistance of some pantomimes, as the *Necromancer, Harlequin Sorcerer, Apollo and Daphne, &c.*, been more frequented than at any time since it was opened. In the year 1727-28 was offered to the public, a piece which was so eminently successful as since to have introduced a new species of drama, the Comic Opera, and therefore deserves particular notice.

On the 29th January, 1728, *The Beggar's Opera* was acted for the first time. We are told, that when Gay shewed this performance to his patron, the Duke of Queensbury, his Grace's observation was, "This is a very odd thing, Gay, it is either a very good thing, or a bad thing." It proved the former, beyond the warmest expectation of the Author or his friends ; though Quin, whose knowledge of the public taste cannot be questioned, was so doubtful of its success, that he refused the part of Macheath, which was therefore given to Walker. It was performed sixty-two nights, and the receipts of the house were higher than ever were known before. From the offer of the part of Macheath to Quin, and the choice afterwards of Walker, it is evident that it was not thought necessary that the performer should be a first-rate singer. Two years afterwards, 19th March,1729-30, Mr. Quin had the *Beggar's Opera* for his benefit, and performed the part of Macheath himself, and received the sum of £206 9s. 6d., which was several pounds more than any one night at the common prices had been produced at that Theatre. His benefit the preceding year brought him only £102 18s. 0d., and the succeeding only £129 3s. 0d.,

The season of 1727-8 had been so occupied by *The Beggar's Opera*, that no new piece was exhibited in which Mr. Quin performed. In that of 1728-29, he performed in Barford's *Virgin Queen ;* in Madden's *Themistocles;* and in Mrs. Heywood's *Frederick Duke of Brunswick*. In 1729-30 there was no new play in which he performed. In 1730-31, he assisted in Tracey's

Periander ; in Frowde's *Philotas ;* in Jeffrey's *Merope ;* and in Theobald's *Orestes ;* and in the next season, 1731-32, in Kelly's *Married Philosopher.*

On the 7th December, 1732, Covent Garden Theatre was opened, and the Company belonging to Lincoln's Inn Fields removed thither. In the course of this season Mr. Quin was called upon to exercise his talents in singing, and accordingly performed Lycomedes, in Gay's posthumous opera of *Achilles,* eighteen nights. The next season concluded his service at Covent Garden. At this juncture the deaths of Wilkes, Booth, and Oldfield, and the succession of Cibber, had thrown the management of Drury Lane Theatre into raw and unexperienced hands. Mr. Highmore, a gentleman of fortune, who had been tempted to intermeddle in it, had sustained so great a loss, as to oblige him to sell his interest to the best bidder. By this event the Drury Lane Theatre came into the possession of Charles Fleetwood, Esq, who, it is said, purchased it in concert with, and at the recommendation of Mr. Rich. But a difference arising between these gentlemen, the former determined to seduce from his antagonist his best performer, and the principal support of his Theatre. Availing himself of this quarrel, Mr. Quin left Covent Garden, and in the beginning of the season 1734-35, removed to the rival theatre, "on such terms," says a writer who seems to be well informed "as no hired actor had before received."

From the time of Mr. Quin's establishment at Drury Lane, until the appearance of Mr. Garrick, in 1741, he was generally allowed the foremost rank in his profession. The elder Mills, who succeeded to Booth, was declining; and Millward, an actor of some merit, had not risen to the height of his excellence, which however, was not at the best very great ; and Boheme was dead. His only competitor seems to have been Delane, whose merits were lost in indolent indulgence. The writer already quoted has drawn the character of this actor, compared with Mr. Quin, in so impartial a manner, that it may not be impertinent to introduce it in this place :—

" Quin, at Drury Lane house, and Delane, at Covent Garden, are the *personæ dramatis* which are without competitors. They both play the chief characters in the same cast, therefore I shall consider their different characters together. Quin has been many years on the stage, and has gradually rose up to that height of reputation he at present enjoys. When Drury Lane was under the direction of the late Mr. Rich, he was in the inferior class, and the Lieutenant of the Tower, in Cibber's alteration of *Richard the Third*, was one of the principal parts he performed. The cast of several plays in print, fully prove his abilities were then thought very insignificant; however, on a new company setting up at Licoln's Inn Fields, he was engaged in it, and has ever since, but more especially on the death of Boheme, gradually rose to a great degree of favour with the public. Mr. Booth's quitting the Stage still set him in a fairer light, and indeed left him without a rival. He had for some time appeared without any competitor, when all on a sudden there appeared at Goodman's Fields, a young tragedian from Dublin. This was Delane. Novelty, youth, a handsome figure, took off from any severe criticism on his elocution and action. In short, though so far from the polite end of the town, he drew to him several polite audiences, and became in such a degree of repute, that comparisons were made between him and Quin; nor was he without admirers of both sexes who gave him the preference. He was not insensible of this, and determined to leave Goodman's Fields, and indulge his ambition at one of the Theatres Royal. Quin just at that time left Covent Garden for Drury Lane, and he engaged with Mr. Rich, at Covent Garden, and in two or three years on the stage, gained that station on it, which most of the other actors could not in many years attain to. Quin has the character of a just speaker, but then it is confined to the solemn declamatory way: he either cannot work himself into the emotions of a violent passion, or he will not take the fatigue of doing it. The partiality of his friends says, he can touch the passions with great delicacy *if he will*; but general opinion affirms, that he has neither power of voice or sensation to give love or pity, grief or remorse, their proper tone and variation of features. Delane is also esteemed a just player; and though he has often a more loud violence of voice, yet either from an imitation of Quin, or his own natural manner, he has a sameness of tone and expression, and drawls out his lines to a displeasing length; but that loud violence of voice is useful to him when anger, indignation, or such enraged passions are to be expressed, for the shrill loudness marks the passion, which the sweet cadence of Quin's natural voice is unequal to. In such parts, especially Alexander, Delane pleases many; for the million, as Colley Cibber says, are apt to be transported when the drum of the ear is soundly rattled. But, on the contrary, Quin's solemn sameness of pronunciation, which conveys an awful dignity, is charmingly affecting in Cato. Delane is young enough to rise to greater perfection; Quin may be said now to be at the height of his: if Delane has the more pleasing person, Quin has the more affecting action; both might soon appear with more advantage,

if they were on the same stage.   The rivalship of Delane would
give a spirited jealousy to Quin, and force him to exert himself;
and Quin's judgment would improve the unfinished action of
Delane; but they are the Cæsar and Pompey of the Theatres,
and one stage would be imcompatible with their ambition; Quin
could bear no one on the footing of an equal, Delane no one as a
superior.

In the year 1735, *Aaron Hill*, in a periodical paper, called *The
Prompter*, attacked some of the principal actors of the stage, and
particularly *Colley Cibber*, and Mr. Quin.   Cibber, says Mr.
Davies, laughed, but Quin was angry; and meeting Mr. Hill in
the Court of Requests, a scuffle ensued between them, which
ended in the exchange of a few blows.

The following seems to be the paragraph which gave offence to
the Actor : "And as to you Mr. All-weight, you lose the advantages of your deliberate articulation, distinct use of pausing,
solemn significance, and that composed air and gravity of your
motion ; for though there arises from all these good qualities an
esteem that will continue and increase the number of your friends,
yet those among them who wish best to your interest, will be
always uneasy at observing perfection so nearly within your reach,
and your spirits not disposed to stretch out and take possession.
To be always *deliberate* and solemn is an error, as certainly,
though not as unpardonably, as *never* to be so.   To pause where
no pauses are necessary, is the way to destroy their effect when
the sense stands in need of their assistance.   And, though dignity is finely maintained by the weight of majestic composure,
yet are there scenes in your parts where the voice should be
sharp and impatient, the look disordered and agonized, the action
precipitate and turbulent ; for the sake of such difference as we
see in some smooth canal, where the stream is scarce visible compared with the other end of the same canal, rushing rapidly down
a cascade, and breaking beauties which owe their attraction to
violence."

Mr. Quin was hardly settled at Drury Lane before he became
embroiled in a dispute relative to *Mons. Poitier* and *Madame
Roland*, then two celebrated dancers, whose neglect of duty it
had fallen to his lot to apologise for.   On the 12th December,
the following advertisement appeared in the newspapers :—

"Whereas on Saturday last, the audience of the Theatre Royal,
in Drury Lane, was greatly incensed at their disappointment in
M. Poitier and Madame Roland's not dancing, as their names
were in the bills for the day, and Mr. Quin, seeing no way to
appease the resentment then shown, but by relating the real

F

messages sent from the Theatre to know the reasons why they did not come to perform, and the answers returned. And whereas there were two advertisements in the Daily Post of Tuesday last, insinuating that Mr. Quin, had with malice accused the said Poitier and Madame Roland: I therefore think it (in justice to Mr. Quin) incumbent on me to assure the public, that Mr. Quin has conducted himself in this point towards the above mentioned, with the strictest regard to truth and justice, and as Mr. Quin has acted in this affair in my behalf, I think myself obliged to return him thanks for so doing."—CHARLES FLEETWOOD.

After this declaration, no further notice seems to have been taken of the fracas. A short time afterwards the delinquent dancers made their apology to the public, and were received into favour.

In the season of 1734-35, Mr. Quin performed in Lillo's *Christian Hero*, and Fielding's *Universal Gallant;* and in the succeeding one, he first performed Falstaff in the second part of *Henry IV.*, for his own benefit. In 1736-37, he performed in Miller's *Universal Passion*, and in 1737-38, in the same author's *Art and Nature*. It was in this season also, that he performed *Comus* and had the first opportunity of promoting the interest of his friend Thomson, in the tragedy of *Agamemnon*.

The author of *The Actor*, (Dr. Hill) 1755, p. 235, says: "In this Mr. Quin by the force of dignity alone, hid all his natural defects, and supported the part at such a height, that none have been received in it since.

> ' The star that bids the shepherd fold,
> Now the top of heaven doth hold.'

are lines which, though beautiful, have nothing of natural greatness, but Mr. Quin made darkness as he spoke them. The solemnity and enthusiasm with which he pronounced them, called up the idea of a still and dead midnight, more than all the descriptions even of Milton. When he afterwards delivered,

> ' The sounds, the seas, and all their finny drove,
> Now to the moon in wav'ring morrice move ;'

so strong was the imagery he added to the strength already given by the poet, that we saw the curled waves break in upon the calm repose of the night, and the peaceful fishes rising and falling under their indented motion. When he afterwards, with that change of tone and cadence which he possessed beyond all mortal men (spite of the charge of his monotony) added,

> ' While on the tawney sands and shelves,
> Trip the pert fairies and the dapper elves,'

we smiled and shook, and saw the little beings

> ' Whose midnight revels, by a forest side,
> Or fountain, some belated peasant sees,
> Or dreams he sees; while overhead the moon
> Sits arbitress, and nearer to the earth
> Wheels her pale course.'

His invocation of Cotytto was masterly beyond all these. It was not delivered with awe and humility, as men address their prayers; for it was not of a mortal to a Deity, but a superior nature addressing another, nothing more than equal:

> ' Hail, Goddess of nocturnal sport,
> Dark veil'd Cotytto, t' whom the secret flame
> Of midnight torches burn.
> —Stay thy cloudy ebon chair.'

There was in this all the solemnity and serious attention of a prayer, though nothing of the confessed inferiority; we glowed, we trembled with delight and terror as his deep voice pronounced it. He rose upon his audience through the whole course of this great character, and at the last, when to the lady who would rise and leave him, he said,

> ' Nay, lady sit ! If I but wave this wand,
> Your nerves are all bound up in alabaster,
> And you a statue ; or, as Daphne was,
> Root-bound, that fled Apollo.'

we heard the greatest sentence ever pronounced upon the British theatre. Throughout the part he courts not as a mortal, but as a superior power, by promises, not entreaties, and when at the last he proceeds to threats, the poet has not more happily chosen his words than this player pronounced them.

There was in all this very little of gesture: the look, the elevated posture, and the brow of majesty, did all. This was most just ; for as the hero of tragedy exceeds the gentleman of comedy, and therefore in his general deportment is to use fewer gestures ; the deity of the Masque exceeds the hero in dignity, and therefore is to be yet more sparing.

Again, the language of Milton, the most sublime of any in our tongue, seemed formed for the mouth of this player, and he did justice to the sentiments, which in that author are always equal to the language. If he was a hero in *Pyrrhus*, he was as it became him, in *Comus* a demi-god. Mr. Quin was old when he performed this part, and his natural manner grave; he was therefore unfit in common things for a youthful God of Revels, yet did he command our attention and applause in the part in spite of these and all his other disadvantages. In the place of youth he had dignity, and for vivacity he gave us grandeur. The author has connected them in the character, and whatever young and spirited player shall attempt it after him, we shall remember his manner, faulty as it was, in what he could not help; in what nature, not want of judgment, misrepresented it, so as to set the other in contempt.

The season of 1738-39, produced only one new play in which Mr. Quin performed, and that was *Mustapha*, by Dr. Mallet, which, according to Mr. Davies, was said to glance both at the King and Sir Robert Walpole, in the characters of Solyman the Magnificent, and Rustan, his Vizier.

On the first night of its exhibition were assembled all the chiefs in opposition to the Court; and many speeches were applied by the audience to the supposed grievances of the times, and to persons and characters. The play was in general well acted, more particularly the parts of Solyman and Mustapha by Quin and Milward. Mr. Pope was present in the boxes, and at the end of the play went behind the scenes, a place which he had not visited for some years. He expressed himself to be well pleased with his entertainment; and particularly addressed himself to Quin, who was greatly flattered with the distinction paid him by so great a man; and when Pope's servant brought his master's scarlet cloak, Quin insisted upon the honour of putting it on.

In the season of 1739-40, there was acted at Drury Lane theatre, on the 12th of November, a tragedy entitled, *The Fatal Retirement*, by a Mr. Anthony Brown, which received its sentence of condemnation on the first night. In this play Mr. Quin had been solicited to perform which he refused, and the ill success which attended the piece irritated the author and his friends so much, that they ascribed its failure to the absence of Mr. Quin, and in consequence of it, repeatedly insulted him for several nights afterwards when he appeared on the stage. This treatment at length Mr. Quin resented and determined to repel. Coming forward therefore, he addressed the audience, and informed them, that at the request of the author he had read his piece before it was acted, and given him his very sincere opinion of it; that it was the very worst play he had ever read in his life, and for that reason had refused to act in it. This spirited explanation was received with great applause, and for the future entirely silenced the opposition to him. In this season he performed in Lillo's *Elmerick*.

On the 1st of August, 1740, an entertainment of a peculiar kind was given by Frederick Prince of Wales, father of his present Majesty, in the gardens of Cliefden, in commemoration of the accession of King George the First, and in honour of the birth of the Princess Augusta, now Duchess of Brunswick. It consisted of the *Masque of Alfred*, by Thomson and Mallet ; the *Masque of the Judgment of Paris ;* and some scenes from Rich's *Pantomimes*, by him and Lalauze, with dancing by Signora Barbarini, then lately arrived from Paris. The whole was exhibited upon a theatre in the garden composed of vegetables, and decorated with festoons of flowers, at the end of which was erected a pavilion for the Prince and Princess of Wales, Prince George (his present Majesty) and Princess Augusta. The performers in *Alfred* were Quin, who represented the Hermit, Milward, Mills, Salway, Mrs. Clive, and Mrs. Horton. "The accommodation for the company," says Mr. Davies, "I was told, was but scanty and ill-managed, and the players were not treated as persons ought to be who are employed by a Prince. Quin, I believe was admitted among those of the higher order ; and Mrs. Clive might be safely trusted to take care of herself anywhere." The whole of the entertainment concluded with fireworks made by Dr. Desaguliers.

The next season, that of 1740-41, concluded Mr. Quin's engagement at Drury Lane. In that period no new play was produced ; but on the revival of *As You Like It*, and *The Merchant of Venice*, he performed for the first time, the parts of Jacques and Antonio, having declined the part of the Jew, which was offered to him, and accepted by Mr. Macklin. The irregular conduct of the manager, Mr. Fleetwood, was this time such, that it can excite but little surprise that a man like Mr. Quin should find his situation so uneasy as to be induced to relinquish it. In the summer of 1741, Mr. Quin, Mrs. Clive, Mr. Ryan, and Mademoiselle Chateauneuf, then esteemed the best female dancer in Europe, made an excursion to Dublin. Mr. Quin had been there before, in the month of June, 1739, accompanied by Mr. Giffard, and received at his benefit £126, at that time esteemed a great sum.

On this second visit, Mr. Quin opened in his favourite part of Cato, to as crowded an audience as the theatre could contain. Mrs. Clive next appeared in Lappet in the *Miser*. She certainly was one of the best that ever played it. And Mr. Ryan came forward in Iago, to Mr. Quin's Othello. With such excellent performers, we may naturally suppose the plays were admirably sustained. Perhaps it will scarcely be credited, that so finished a comic actress as Mrs. Clive could so far mistake her abilities, as to play Lady Townly, to Mr. Quin's Lord Townly and Mr. Ryan's Manly ; Cordelia to Mr. Quin's Lear, and Ryan's Edgar, &c. However, she made ample amends by her performance of Nell, the Virgin Unmasked, the Country Wife, and Euphrosyne in *Comus*, which was got up on purpose, and acted for the first time in Ireland.

Mr. Quin seems to have attended the Dublin Company to Cork and Limerick, and the next season, 1741-42, we find him performing in Dublin, where he acted the part of Justice Balance, in *The Recruiting Officer*, at the opening of the theatre in October, on a Government night. He afterwards performed Jacques, Apemantus, Richard, Cato, Sir John Brute and Falstaff, unsupported by any performer of eminence. In December however Mrs. Cibber arrived, and performed Indiana to his Young Bevil, and afterwards they were frequently in the same play, as in Chamont and Monimia, in *The Orphan*; Comus and the Lady ; Duke and Isabella, in *Measure for Measure ;* Friar and Queen, in *The Spanish Friar ;* Horatio and Calista, in *The Fair Penitent, &c.*, with uncommon applause, and generally to crowded houses. The state of the Irish stage was then so low, that it was often found that the whole receipts of the house were not more than sufficient to discharge Mr. Quin's engagement ; and so attentive was he to his own interest, and so rigid in demanding its execution, that we are told by good authority he refused to let the curtains be drawn up until the money was regularly brought to him.

He left Dublin, in February, 1741-2, and on the 25th of March, assisted the widow and four children of Milward, the actor, (who died the 6th of February preceding) and performed Cato at Drury Lane for their benefit. On his arrival in London, he found the attention of the theatrical public entirely occupied by the merits of Mr. Garrick, who in the October preceding had begun his theatrical career, and was then performing with prodigious success at Goodman's-fields. The fame of the new performer afforded no pleasure to Mr. Quin, who sarcastically observed, that " Garrick was a new religion, and that Whitefield was followed for a time ; but they would all come to church again." This observation being communicated to Mr. Garrick, he wrote the following epigram :—

> Pope *Quin* who damns all churches but his own,
> Complains that heresy corrupts the town :
> That Whitefield *Garrick* has misled the age,
> " Schism " he cries, " has turned the nation's brain,
> But eyes will open, and to church again ! "

> Thou great Infallible, forbear to roar,
> Thy bulls and errors are rever'd no more;
> When doctrines meet with general approbation,
> It is not heresy, but reformation.

In the season of 1742-43, Mr. Quin returned to his former master, Rich, at Covent Garden Theatre, where he opposed Mr. Garrick at Drury Lane, it must be added with very little success. But though the applause the latter obtained from the public was not agreeable to Mr. Quin, yet we find that a scheme was proposed and agreed to, though not carried into execution, in the summer of 1743, for them to perform together for their mutual benefit a few nights at Lincoln's Inn Fields Theatre. On the failure of this plan Mr. Quin went to Dublin, where he had the mortification to find the fame of Mr. Sheridan, then new to the stage, more adverse to him than even Mr. Garrick's had been in London. Instead of making a profitable bargain in Dublin, as he hoped, he found the managers of the theatres there entirely indisposed to admit him. After staying there a short time he returned to London, without effecting the purpose of his journey, and in no good humour with the new performers.

The season of 1743-44, Mr. Quin, we believe, passed without any engagement, but in that of 1744-45, he was at Covent Garden again, and performed King John, in Cibber's *Papal Tyranny*. The next year seems to have been devoted to repose—whether from indolence, or inability to obtain the terms he required from the managers, is not very apparent. Both may have united. It was some of these periods of relaxation that gave occasion to his friend Thomson, who had been gradually writing the *Castle of Indolence*, for 14 or 15 years, to introduce him into the *Mansion of Idleness*, in this stanza:—

> Here whilom digg'd th' Esopus of the age;
>   But call'd by Fame, in soul ypricked deep,
> A noble pride restor'd him to the stage,
>   And roused him like a giant from his sleep.
> Even from his slumbers we advantage reap,
>   With double force th' enliven'd scene he wakes,
> Yet quits not Nature's bounds. He knows to keep
>   Each due decorum; Now the heart he shakes,
> And now with well urg'd sense th' enlightened judgment takes.

He had the next season, 1746-47, occasion to exert himself, being engaged at Covent Garden, along with Mr. Garrick. It is not, perhaps, says Mr. Davies, more difficult to settle the covenants of a league between mighty monarchs, than to adjust the preliminaries of a treaty in which the high and potent princes of a theatre are the parties. Mr. Garrick and Mr. Quin had too much sense and temper to squabble about trifles. After one or two previous and friendly meetings, they selected such characters as they intended to act, without being obliged to join in the same play. Some parts were to be acted alternately, particularly Richard III., and Othello. The same writer adds: Mr. Quin soon found that his competition with Mr. Garrick, whose reputation was hourly increasing, whilst his own was on the decline, would soon become ineffectual. His Richard the Third could scarce draw together a decent appearance of company in the boxes, and he was with some difficulty tolerated in the part, when Garrick acted the same character to crowded houses, and with very great applause.

The town had often wished to see these great actors fairly matched in two characters of almost equal importance. *The Fair Penitent* presented an opportunity to display their several merits, though it must be owned that the balance was as much in favor of Quin, as the advocate of virtue is superior in argument to the defender of profligacy.

The shouts of applause when Horatio and Lothario met on the stage together (14th Nov. 1746) in the second act, were so loud and so often repeated, before the audience permitted them to speak, that the combatants seemed to be disconcerted. It was observed that Quin changed colour, and Garrick seemed to be embarrassed; and it must be owned, that these actors were never less masters of themselves than on the first night of the contest for pre-eminence. Quin was too proud to own his feelings on the occasion, but Mr. Garrick was heard to say, "'Faith, I believe Quin was as frightened as myself."

The play was repeatedly acted, and with constant applause, to very brilliant audiences; nor is it to be wondered at, for besides the novelty of seeing the two rival actors in the same tragedy, the Fair Penitent was admirably played by Mrs. Cibber.

It was in this season that Mr. Garrick produced *Miss in her Teens*, the success of which is said by Mr. Davies, to have caused no small mortification to Mr. Quin. He however did not think it prudent to refuse Mr. Garrick's offer of performing at his benefit, and accordingly the following letter was prefixed to all Mr. Quin's advertisements :—

Sir,—I am sorry that my present bad state of health makes me uncapable of performing so long and so laborious a character as Jaffier this season. If you think my playing in the farce will be of the least service to you, or any entertainment to the audience, you may command   *Your humble servant,*

March 25th.   *D. GARRICK.*

It was this season also in which *The Suspicious Husband* appeared. The part of Mr. Strickland was offered to Mr. Quin, but he refused it, and in consequence it fell to the lot of Mr. Bridgewater, who obtained great reputation by his performance of it.

Davies in his life of Garrick remarks further : Notwithstanding the disparity arising from one actor pleading the cause of truth and virtue, and the other being engaged on the side of licentiousness and libertinism, Mr. Quin was in the opinion of the best judges, fairly defeated ; by striving to do too much, he missed the mark at which he aimed. The character of Horatio is compounded of deliberate courage, warm friendship, and cool contempt of insolence. The last Quin had in a superior degree, but could not rise to an equal expression of the other two.

The strong emphasis which he stamped on almost every word in a line robbed the whole of that ease and graceful familiarity which should have accompanied the elocution and action of a man who is calmly chastising a vain and audacious boaster. When Lothario gave Horatio the challenge, Quin instead of accepting it instantaneously, with the determined and unembarrassed brow of superior bravery, made a long pause and dragged out the words

" I'll meet thee there ! "

in such a manner as to make it appear absolutely ludicrous. He paused so long before he spoke, that somebody, it was said, called out from the gallery, "Why don't you tell the gentleman whether you will meet him or not?"

In March 1748 happened the dreadful fire in Cornhill, which gave Mr. Quin an opportunity of displaying his readiness to succour distress. On the 6th of April, he performed *Othello*, at Covent Garden, for the benefit of the sufferers (having come on purpose from Bath) which produced £218 12s. 4d. Soon afterwards he had a benefit himself. On the 27th of August, he lost his friend Thomson, and for the season of 1748-49, he enlisted again under the banners of Rich. On the 13th of January, 1748-49, the tragedy of *Coriolanus* was produced at Covent Garden, in which Mr. Quin played the principal character, and spoke Lord Lyttelton's celebrated prologue, which says Cibber, or Shiells, had a very happy effect on the audience. Mr. Quin was the particular friend of Thomson, and when he spoke the following lines, which are in themselves very tender, all the endearments of a long acquaintance rose at once to his imagination, while the tears gushed from his eyes :

> He lov'd his friends (forgive this gushing tear,
> Alas! I feel I am no actor here)—
> He lov'd his friends with such a warmth of heart,
> So clear of interest, so devoid of art,
> Such generous freedom, such unshaken zeal,
> No words can speak it, but our tears may tell.

The beautiful break in these lines had a fine effect in speaking; Mr. Quin here excelled himself; he never appeared a greater actor than at this instant, when he declared himself none—it was an exquisite stroke of nature, art alone could hardly reach it. Pardon the digression reader, but we feel a desire to say something more on this head. The poet and the actor were friends— it cannot then be quite foreign from the purpose to proceed. A deep-fetched sigh filled up the heartfelt pause, grief spread o'er all the countenance; the tear started to the eye, the muscles fell, and

> " The whiteness of his cheek
> Was apter than his tongue to speak his tale."

They all expressed the tender feelings of a manly heart, becoming a Thomson's friend. His pause, his recovery, were masterly, and he delivered the whole with an emphasis and pathos worthy the excellent lines he spoke; worthy the great poet and good man whose merits they painted, and whose loss they deplored. This account is confirmed by Mr. Murdoch, the writer of Thomsons's life, who says : "My Lord Lyttelton's prologue was admired as one of the best that had ever been written ; the best spoken it certainly was. The sympathising audience saw, that then indeed Mr. Quin was no actor, that the tears he shed were those of real friendship and grief." Dr. Johnson also observes, mentioning this prologue : "that Quin who had long lived with Thomson in fond intimacy, spoke it in such a manner, as showed him to be on that occasion no actor."

Just before the performance of *Coriolanus* an honour had been conferred upon Mr. Quin, which he some years after recollected with no small degree of exultation. On the 4th of January, *Cato* was performed at Leicester House, by the direction of Frederick Prince of Wales, in which his present Majesty, Prince Edward, Princess Augusta, and Princess Elizabeth acted the parts of Portius, Juba, Marcia, and Lucia. The instruction of the young performers and the conduct of the rehearsals were given to Mr. Quin, and if we are not mistaken, he was afterwards rewarded with a pension for his service. It was intended that *Lady Jane Grey* should have been represented by the same performers, and accordingly that play was revived at Covent Garden, in Dec. 1750, but for some reason the intended exhibition did not take place.

When Mr. Quin heard of the graceful manner in which his Majesty repeated his first speech to his parliament, he cried out, "Aye, I taught the boy to speak!" Prince Frederick, perhaps through the means of Thomson and Lyttelton, was a warm patron of Mr. Quin. He generally used to attend his benefit, and all the plays he commanded, unless on some very particular occasion, were confined to Covent Garden Theatre, in compliment to this actor. This attention in his royal highness was so beneficial to Mr. Quin, that his salary in the last season of his performance, we are told was equal to a thousand pounds.

We are now arrived at that period. The season of 1750-51 opened with a very powerful company at Covent Garden, consisting of Mr. Barry, Mrs. Cibber, Mr. Quin, Mrs. Woffington, Mr. Macklin, &c. The combined strength of this assemblage of theatrical talents, it is said alarmed Mr. Garrick so much, that he wished to detach Mr. Quin from the party, but having had the command at Covent Garden, he did not wish to be controlled by Mr. Garrick; he therefore continued with his old master, Rich, upon higher terms than had ever been paid to any actor. His benefit was on the 18th of March, three days before the death of the Prince of Wales, by whose command, though he was not present at the performance, *Othello* was acted : Othello by Mr. Barry; Iago, Mr. Quin; and Desdemona, Mrs. Cibber. It is recorded that notwithstanding the novelty of this change in the performers, Othello being Quin's usual part, the house was by no means a crowded one, on the contrary it was very thinly attended. On the 20th May, Mr. Quin performed Horatio, in *The Fair Penitent*, and with that character concluded his performances as a hired actor.

By the retirement of Mr. Quin the stage sustained a great loss, the characters in which he particularly excelled falling into the hands of actors whose talents were very inadequate to their proper representation. In his principal tragic parts he was succeeded by Sparks, but in the character of Falstaff he left no representative. As Mr. Garrick in a prologue to *Florizel and Perdita*, spoken in 1756, at Drury Lane, truly observed,

"But should you call for Falstaff, where to find him,
He's gone, nor left one cup of sack behind him.
Sunk in his elbow chair, no more he'll roam,
No more with merry wags to Eastcheap come ;
He's gone—to jest, and laugh, and give his sack at home."

Mr. Quin had always been attentive to the dictates of prudence, which enabled him to assert a character of independence while he

continued on the stage, and secured to him a competent provision
when he quitted it.

In 1761, his theatrical abilities were again canvassed by the
frequenters of the theatres, on the occasion of Mr. Churchill's
introducing him into the *Rosciad*, in the following manner :

> " Quin from afar, lur'd by the scent of fame,
> A Stage Leviathan, put in his claim,
> Pupil of Betterton and Booth.   Alone,
> Sullen he walk'd, and deem'd the chair his own ;
> For how should moderns, mushrooms of the day,
> Who ne'er those masters knew, know how to play ?
> Grey-bearded veterans, who with partial tongue
> Extol the times when they themselves were young,
> Who, having lost all relish for the Stage,
> See not their own defects, but lash the age,
> Receiv'd with joyful murmurs of applause
> Their darling chief, and lin'd his fav'rite cause.

> " Far be it from the candid Muse to tread
> Insulting o'er the ashes of the dead,
> But, just to living merit, she maintains,
> And dares the test whilst Garrick's genius reigns,
> Ancients in vain endeavour to excel,
> Happily prais'd, if they could act as well.
> But though prescription's force we disallow,
> Nor to antiquity submissive bow ;
> Tho' we deny imaginary grace,
> Founded on accidents of time and place,   •
> Yet real worth of ev'ry growth shall bear
> Due praise, nor must we, Quin, forget thee there.

> " His words bore sterling weight, nervous and strong,
> In manly tides of sense they roll'd along ;
> Happy in art, he chiefly had pretence
> To keep up numbers, yet not forfeit sense,
> No actor ever greater heights could reach,
> In all the labour'd artifice of speech.

> "Speech ! Is that all ? And shall an actor found
> An universal fame on partial ground ;
> Parrots themselves speak properly by rote,
> And in six months my dog shall howl by note.
> I laugh at those who, when the stage they tread,
> Neglect the heart to compliment the head ;
> With strict propriety their care's confin'd
> To weigh out words, while passion halts behind ;
> To syllable dissectors they appeal,
> Allow them accent, cadence—fools may feel ;
> But, spite of all the criticising elves,
> Those who would make us feel must feel themselves.

> " His eyes, in gloomy sockets taught to roll,
> Proclaim'd the sullen habit of his soul :

Heavy and phlegmatic he trode the stage,
Too proud for tenderness, too dull for rage.
When Hector's lovely widow shines in tears,
Or Rowe's gay rake dependent virtue jeers,
With the same cast of features he is seen
To chide the libertine, and court the queen.
From the tame scene, which without passion flows ;
With just desert his reputation rose ;
Nor less he pleas'd when on some surly plan
He was at once the actor and the man.

" In Brute, he shone unequall'd ;—all agree,
Garrick's not half so great a brute as he.
When Cato's labour'd scenes are brought to view,
With equal praise the actor labour'd too ;
For still you'll find, trace passions to their root,
Small diff'rence 'twixt the stoic and the brute.
In fancy'd scenes, as in life's real plan,
He could not for a moment sink the man.
In whate'er cast his character was laid,
Self still, like oil, upon the surface play'd.
Nature, in spite of all his skill, crept in,
Horatio, Dorax, Falstaff—still was Quin."

Quin's last appearance was at Covent Garden Theatre (for the benefit of Ryan) March 19th, 1753, in the first part of Shakespeare's *Henry IV.*, when his success was so great (according to Mrs. Bellamy) that Ryan was induced to solicit the same favour again the next year, a request however then declined for a reason already alluded to, viz., the loss of his teeth, which drew from him the reply, that "he would play for Tom if he could, but would not *whistle* Falstaff for him."

Quin was a man of strong, pointed sense, with strong passions, and a bad temper ; yet in good humour was an excellent companion and better bred than many who valued themselves upon good manners. 'Tis true when he drank freely, which was often the case, he forgot himself, and there was a sediment of brutality in him when you shook the bottle ; but he made you ample amends by his pleasantry and good sense when he was sober. He told a story admirably and concisely, and his expressions were strongly marked ; however he often had an assumed character, and spoke in blank verse, which procured him respect from some, but exposed him to ridicule from others, who had discernment to see through his pomp and affectation. He was sensual and loved good eating, but not so much as was generally reported with some exaggeration, and he was luxurious in his descriptions of those turtle and venison feasts, to which he was invited. He was, in his dealings, a very honest, fair man ; yet he understood his interest, and knew how to deal with the managers, and never made a bad bargain with them, in truth it was not an easy matter to overeach a man of his capacity and penetration, united with a knowledge of mankind.		He was not so much an ill-natured as an ill-humoured man, and he was capable of friendship. His airs of importance, and his gait, were absurd; so that he might be said to walk in blank verse as well as talk; but his good sense corrected him, and he did not continue long in the fits. I have heard him represented as a cringing fawning fellow to lords and great men, but I could never discover that mean disposition in him.		I observed he was decent and respectful in high company, and had a very proper behaviour, without arrogance or diffidence, which made him more circumspect, and consequently less entertaining.

Of Quin's generosity of disposition and readiness to help in all cases of need that came under his notice, we give in addition to what has already been mentioned, the following:—

During the time he had the chief direction at Covent Garden Theatre (says Mrs. Bellamy) he revived *The Maid's Tragedy*, written by Beaumont and Fletcher. In it he played the character of Melanthus, Mrs. Pritchard, Evandra, and myself Aspasia. One day after the rehearsal was finished, he desired to speak with me in his dressing room.		As he had always carefully avoided seeing me alone, I was not a little surprised at so unexpected an invitation.		My apprehensions even made me fear that I had, by some means or other, offended a man, whom I really loved as a father.		My fears however were not of long duration, for as soon as I had entered the dressing room, he took me by the hand, with a smile of ineffable benignity, and thus addressed me : " My dear girl ! you are vastly followed I hear.		Do not let the love of finery, or any other inducement, prevail upon you to commit an indiscretion.		Men in general are rascals.		You are young and engaging, and therefore ought to be doubly cautious. If you want anything in my power which money can purchase, come to me, and say, ' James Quin, give me such a thing,' and my purse shall be always at your service."		The tear of gratitude stood in my eye, at this noble instance of generosity ; and his own glistened with that of humanity and self-approbation.

Again :—Winstone once had a quarrel with his manager, and abruptly leaving London, contrary to the advice of Quin, went strolling into Wales. After two years' absence, on his return from Swansea to Bristol, by sea, he was near being drowned in a storm which stranded the ship, by which he lost all his clothes, and what little money he had.		In this situation he scrambled to London, and getting to one of his old haunts about the Garden, went to bed, and sulked for two days without ever getting out of it. Quin, by accident, heard of his situation, and immediately calling on the manager, had Winstone put on his usual salary, and his name actually advertised in the bills for the next day's performance. He then went to Monmouth-street, and bought him a full suit of clothes. Thus provided, Quin called upon his old friend, whom he found in bed very melancholy. After some conversation, Quin asked Winstone why he was not at rehearsal ? This at first astonished him, till the other explaining the circumstance, he fell upon his knees with gratitude.—" But zounds, my dear Jemmy," says Winstone, "what shall I do for clothes, and a little money !" "As for the clothes," says Quin, "there they are : but as for money, by G–d you must put your hand into *your own pocket.*" Winstone upon searching the breeches pocket found ten guineas.

Much has been said about Quin's love of good living, and not a few jokes were uttered at his expense with regard to this feature of his character. Smollett, in his *Humphrey Clinker*, says :— " Quin is a real voluptuary in the articles of eating and drinking ; and so confirmed an epicure, in the common acceptation of the term, that he cannot put up with ordinary fare. This is a point of such importance with him, that he always takes upon himself the charge of catering, and a man admitted to his mess, is always sure of eating delicate victuals and drinking excellent wine. He owns himself addicted to the delights of the stomach, and often jokes upon his own sensuality ; but there is nothing selfish in this appetite. He finds that good cheer unites good company, exhilarates the spirits, opens the heart, banishes all restraint from conversation, and promotes the happiest purposes of social life." A writer, however, in the *St. James's Chronicle,* supposed to be Mr. Victor, soon after Mr. Quin's death, observed :—" Quin certainly loved eating well, as it is called, but he as certainly loved to talk about it much more ; and having gained the reputation of being an epicure, he encouraged it, in talking with goût of venison, John Dory, &c., but of late years, to my certain knowledge, he was no great eater ; I have heard him, indeed, at four o'clock in the morning call for the prime minister of the kitchen, and order a partridge to be salmagundied, but it was merely for the wit in calling for it."

His love of the "John Dory" comes out in many little ways, and was even made the subject of an epitaph. He used to say, it was "not safe to sit down to a turtle feast at one of the city halls without a basket-hilted knife and fork."—Another of his quips was, "Of all the banns of marriage I ever heard, none gave me half such pleasure as the union of Ann-chovy with good John-Dory," and we have the following on his death :—

> "Alas, poor Quin ! thy jests and stories
> Are quite extinguish'd ; and what more is,
> There's no *Jack Falstaff*, no *John Dories*."

Bath, Jan. 21.   W. W.

One writer says : Quin in his old age, became a great gourmand, and among other things, invented a composition which he called his *Siamese soup*, pretending that its ingredients were principally from the East.   The peculiarity of its flavour became the topic of the day.   The *rage* at Bath was Mr. Quin's soup ; but as he would not part with the receipt, this state of notice was highly inconvenient ; every person of taste was endeavouring to dine with him ; every dinner he was at, an apology was made for the absence of the *Siamese soup*.   His female friends Quin was forced to put off with promises ; the males received a respectful but manly denial.   A conspiracy was accordingly projected by a dozen *bon vivants* of Bath, against his peace and comfort.   At home he was flooded with anonymous letters ; abroad beset with applications under every form.   The possession of this secret was made a canker to all his enjoyments.   At length he discovered the design and determined on revenge.   Collecting the names of the principal confederates, he invited them to dinner, promising to give them the receipt before they departed—an invitation which was joyfully accepted.   Quin then gave a pair of his old boots to the housemaid to scour and soak, and when sufficiently seasoned, to chop up into fine particles, like minced meat.   On the appointed day, he took these particles, and pouring them into a copper pot, with sage, onions, spice, ham, wine, water, and other ingredients, composed a mixture of about two gallons, which was served up at his table as *Siamese soup*.   The company were in transports at its flavour, but Quin pleading a cold did not taste it.   A pleasant evening was spent, and when the hour of departure arrived, each person pulled out his tablet to write down the receipt.   Quin now pretended that he had forgot making the promise, but his guests were not to be put off, and closing the door, they told him in plain terms, that neither he nor they should quit the room till his pledge had been redeemed.   Quin stammered and evaded, and kept them from the point as long as possible, but when their patience was bearing down all bounds, his reluctance gave way.   " Well then, gentlemen," said he, "in the first place, take an old pair of boots,"—" What ! an old pair of boots !"—" The older the better."   (They stared at each other) "Cut off their tops and soles, and soak them in a tub of water (they hesitated) chop them into fine particles, and pour them into a pot with two gallons and a half of water."—"Why, Quin," they simultaneously exclaimed, "You do not mean to say that the soup we have been drinking was made of old boots!"—"I do, gentlemen," he replied, "My cook will assure you she chopped them up." They required no such attestation; his cool inflexible expression was sufficient, in an instant horror was depicted in each countenance.

It would be to leave this narrative very incomplete, to conclude it without giving a few samples of the humour for which this actor was so greatly celebrated. Unfortunately most of his jests are of too loose a character to quote in decent society, or to reprint for general reading, but we have selected a few which will shew his nature without giving offence to any.

Macklin having written a comedy many years ago, shewed it to his friend Quin, and asked his opinion of it. Quin gave him some hopes of its success, but desired him to wait a little before he brought it out. His advice was complied with, and the next season he was called upon again for his interest with Mr. Rich, to have it performed; but Quin had the address to satisfy Macklin a second time, by recommending him to wait a little longer. *Shylock* retired growling, but complied. Next year he again applied, confident of success, but was astonished at receiving the same answer as before. Unable to contain himself, he pettishly asked his patron how much longer he would have to wait.—"Till the day of judgment, (replied he,) when you and your play may be d—d together."

FOOTE AND QUIN.—Foote had signified in his advertisements, while he was exhibiting his imitations at one of the Theatres Royal, that he would on a particular evening take off Quin, who, being desirous of seeing his own picture, took a place in the stage box, and when the audience had done applauding Foote for the justness of the representation, Quin bawled out, with a loud horse laugh, "I'm glad on't by G—d; the poor fellow will get a clean shirt by it."—When Foote retorted from the stage, "A clean shirt, Master Quin? that was a very novel thing in your family a few years ago."

To the Master of an Inn who had complained of being infested with rats, he promised a receipt to drive them away. On quitting the house, he had an extravagant bill put into his hands, which he paid; and on the Inkeeper's reminding him of his promise, he returned his bill to him, saying, "Shew them this, and they'll come no more near you, I'll engage."

"Quin and Foote having been invited to Lord Halifax's house

G

at Hampstead, went out to walk, and—but the story is told in
rhyme, and though not new, may be worthy quoting :—

> " As Quin and Foote one day walked out,
>   To view the country round,
> In merry mood they chatting stood,
>   Hard by a village pound.
>
> Foote from his fob a shilling took,
>   And said, ' I'll bet a penny,
> In a small space, near to this place,
>   I'll make this piece a guinea !'
>
> Then on the ground, within the pound
>   The shilling soon was thrown ;
> ' Behold,' said he, ' the thing's made ou¹,
>   For there is one pound one !'
>
> ' I wonder not,' said Quin, ' that thought
>   Should in your head be found,
> For that's the way you pay your debts,
>   A shilling in the pound !' "

"At one time of their acquaintanceship Quin obtained an
ascendancy over Foote, and Foote was afraid to encounter him.
This he had allowed his antagonist to discover, and Quin was not
a man likely to relinquish a victory obtained over a giant. A
coolness in consequence had for some time subsisted between
them, when one afternoon they saw each other under the Piazza
of Covent Garden. They could not avoid meeting, and Quin held
out his hand in token of peace. It was accepted, and they
immediately adjourned to the Shakespeare, ' to enact,' as Quin
said, ' *the play of Measure for Measure.*' They soon became very
jovial, but at last Foote said, ' Quin, I can't be happy till I tell
you one thing.' ' Tell it then, and be happy, Sam.' ' Why,' said
Foote, ' you said I had only one shirt, and that I lay in bed till
it was washed.' ' I never said it, Sam,' replied Quin, ' I never
said it, and I'll soon convince you that I never could have said it
—I never thought you had a shirt to wash.' "

One day at a party in Bath, Quin said something which caused
a general murmur of delighted merriment. A nobleman present,
who was not distinguished for the brilliancy of his ideas,
exclaimed : " What a pity 'tis, Quin, my boy, that a clever fellow
like you should be a player !" Quin, fixing and flashing his eyes
upon the speaker, replied : " Why what would your lordship have
me be ?—a lord ?"

Quin despised and detested theatrical dancers, and having upon
an occasion thrust upon him the disagreeable task of excusing the
non-appearance of a popular danseuse, he executed it by saying :
" I am desired by the manager to inform you that the dance in-

tended for to-night is obliged to be omitted, on account of Madame Rollan having dislocated her ankle. I wish it had been her neck."

A person whom Quin had offended one day met him in the street, and stopped him. "Mr. Quin," said he, "I—I—I understand you have been taking away my name." "What have I said, sir?" "You—you—you called me a scoundrel, sir." "Oh, then keep your name, sir," replied Quin, and walked on.

His sense of fun and satire combined was very great. Witness the ghost trick. He and a friend were passing through St. Paul's Churchyard one evening when their attention was attracted by a mob of people who were listening to a certain man who declared "that there had been a chimney on fire in the borough; that he had seen, with his own eyes, the engines go, in order to extinguish it; but that it was quite got under before the engines arrived." Upon seeing the attention of such a concourse of people attracted by so very unentertaining a detail, Mr. Quin and his friend could not help reflecting upon the natural curiosity of Englishmen, which was excited by the most trifling circumstance;—and very frequently by no circumstance at all. "Let us try," said Quin, "an experiment upon our countrymen's curiosity." This was immediately agreed to; and they repaired to the other side of the churchyard, where, having taken a convenient stand, and staring up the stone gallery, Quin gravely said, "This is about the time." —"Yes," replied the other, taking out his watch, and looking at it under a lamp, "this was precisely the time it made its appearance last night." They had now collected at least a dozen inquisitive spectators, who, fixing their eyes upon the steeple, asked, "What was to be seen?" To this Mr. Quin replied, "that the ghost of a lady who had been murdered had been seen to walk round the rails of the stone-gallery for some evenings, and that she was expected to walk again to-night." This information was presently spread through the multitude, which, by this time, was augmented to a hundred. All eyes were fixed upon the stone-gallery, and imagination frequently supplied the place of reality, in making them believe they saw something move on the top of the balustrade. The joke having thus taken, Quin and his companion withdrew, went and passed the evening at the Half-Moon Tavern, in Cheapside, and upon their return, between twelve and one, the crowd still remained in eager expectation of the ghost's arrival. And yet Quin could say of Macklin, "If God writes a legible hand, that fellow is a villain." At another time, Quin had the hardihood to say to Macklin himself, "Mr. Macklin, by the *lines*—I beg your pardon, sir—by the *cordage* of your face, you should be hanged." It was poor old Macklin who had three pauses in his acting—the first, moderate ; the second, twice as long ; but his last, or " grand pause," as he styled it, was so long, that the prompter, on one occasion, thinking his memory failed, repeated the cue (as it is technically called) several times, and at last so loud as to be heard by the audience. At length Macklin rushed from the stage, and knocked him down, exclaiming, "The fellow interrupted me in my grand pause !"

As Quin was one morning walking near the Lower Rooms in Bath, he was met by a celebrated gambler, who said to him, " So, Mr. Quin, I see you are going to take your ride, to get you an appetite for your dinner."—" Yes," replied Quin, " and you are going to get a dinner to your appetite."

Quin (as Sir George Beaumont told me) was once at a very small dinner party. The master of the house, pushing a delicious pudding towards Quin, begged him to taste it. A gentleman had just before helped himself to an immense piece of it. " Pray," said Quin, looking first at the gentleman's plate and then at the dish, " which *is* the pudding "—*S. Rogers's " Table Talk."*

BON MOT OF QUIN.—One summer, when the month of July happened to be extremely cold, some person asked Quin if he ever remembered such a summer. " Oh yes," replied the wag, " last winter."

QUIN AT THE THREE TUNS.— Quin —who was very stout — was one day coming in a chair from having dined at the Three Tuns, Bath. Lord Chesterfield meeting him, said, " that if Quin came from thence, there were but two tuns left."

ON THE DEATH OF THE LATE MR. QUIN.
Gentleman's Magazine, 1766.

" Says Death to Britannia—' Your great ones you see,
The first in the land, have submitted to me.—
But further prepare now, Britannia to feel
A strike more severe from my conquering steel.'
Then with a malicious and horrible grin,
He drew out an arrow, and shot it at Quin."

Answer to the above Epigram.

" Says Britannia to Death,—' in good faith I don't see
Why the fall of old Quin is so grievous to me !
The loss of a quibble, a pun, or bon mot,
Don't appear to Britannia such matters of woe.
How happy this land, were she never to feel
More fatal effects of your conquering steel !
Much merit he had ; but we've cause to deplore
And of late, the destruction of those who had more,
May his manes in peace and tranquillity sleep,
But let vendors of ven'son, and fish-women weep.' "

A FEW HUMOROUS LINES BY A CONSTANT READER.

Royal Magazine, 1768.

" Are these your Managers ? cries out old Quin :
Fools to fall out—before they well fall in :—
These our Successors ?   These your Play-house Kings !
At loggerheads 'bout two such silly things—
O shame ! to think how much this mushroom race
Of buskin Rulers shall their Thrones disgrace.
If for two straws these Lords such squabbles make
When Fame, when Fortune, everything's at stake.
Where I to come from these dread Shades below,
I'd make these upstart, pigmy Leaders know
How ill their motley characters it suits,
To cram the public with their damn'd disputes ;
I'd let these brawling, wronghead puppies see
How great th' impertinence to disagree :
For well they know their common tasks require
Their powers united, steady and entire :
To teach these School-boys, I, with brother Rich,
Resolve to lash each wrangling youngster's breech,
That they may learn from our correcting hands,
This Rule—A House divided never stands.' "

W. B.

EPITAPH ON MR. QUIN.

Written by Mr. Garrick.

"That tongue, which set the table on a roar
And charm'd the public ear, is heard no more !
Clos'd are those eyes, the harbingers of wit,
Which spoke, before the tongue, what Shakespeare writ,
Cold are those hands, which, living, were stretch'd forth,
At friendship's call, to succour modest worth.
Here lies James Quin ! deign, reader, to be taught,
(Whate'er thy strength of body, force of thought,
In nature's happiest mould however cast,)
To his complexion thou must come at last."

INDEX.

ERRATUM.

Page 12—for 1864 read 1694.

www.ingramcontent.com/pod-product-compliance
Lightning Source LLC
Chambersburg PA
CBHW022144020726
47496CB00008B/2554